BEST FRIENDS' Bakery

Sugar & Spice

Look out for

A Spoonful of Secrets

Sugar & Spice

LINDA CHAPMAN

Illustrated by Kate Hindley

Orion
Children's Books

First published in Great Britain 2014
by Orion Children's Books
a division of the Orion Publishing Group Ltd
Orion House
5 Upper St Martin's Lane
London WC2 9EA
An Hachette UK Company

1 3 5 7 9 10 8 6 4 2

Text © Linda Chapman 2014
Illustrations © Kate Hindley 2014

Printed in Great Britain by Clays Ltd, St Ives plc

ISBN 978 1 4440 1188 3

www.orionbooks.co.uk

To Jenny Glencross, my brilliant and very lovely editor, who first had the idea about the Sugar and Spice Bakery and who has added an infinite amount to the whole series.

Also, to Danny and Sandra Jimminson (from the wonderful Hammer and Pincers in Wymeswold) and Emma Purcell for the baking advice, recipes, encouragement and for always being there whenever I had a question I couldn't answer.

Thank you all so much!

MY BAKING BOOK (and other stuff)

Name: Hannah

Age: $10^{3}/4$

Birthday: 1st August

Likes: baking, drawing, swimming, seeing my friends

Dislikes: spiders and slugs

This is my journal. It's for all sorts of important things - lists, cake designs, cookery facts, a few other things, but most of all for RECIPES!

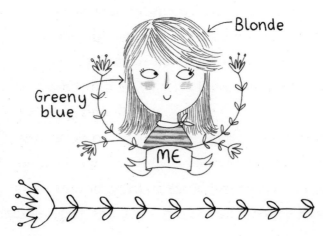

Blonde

Greeny blue

ME

1

When I told my mum she should follow her dreams and open her own bakery, I didn't realise it would mean moving house, leaving all my friends *and* starting a new school. But that's exactly what did happen. The Sugar and Spice Bakery opens tomorrow, and there's only a week until I start my new school. I can't decide which of the two things I'm more nervous about.

The bakery really has to be a success. Mum's given up her office job and spent all her savings, so it just *has* to. It took us ages to choose the name. In the end, we decided on the Sugar and Spice Bakery, because lots of our favourite recipes – such as gingerbread

1

men and cinnamon swirls – have both sugar
and spice in, and it's the combination that
makes them so yummy. I also secretly like the
name because it reminds me of Mum. She's
sweet and lovely to everyone, but she's got
a fiery temper too. Sugar and spice, you see?
She's sort of like a hot cross bun.

OK, I've just compared my mum to a hot
cross bun – I know that's a bit weird, but I
have this thing where I like to imagine what
sort of cake or bun or pastry people I know
might be. Me? I'd be an Eccles cake (which
is a sort of round flaky pastry filled with
currants and with sugar on top). Nothing too
fancy to look at, but nice on the inside. (Or at
least I think I am.)

Anyway, where was I? Oh, the Sugar and Spice Bakery. It feels so scary and different and new and exciting all at the same time. It's like Mum says – sometimes you just have to take a chance and see what happens. It's the same with baking – you can make an ordinary sponge cake every time, or you can take a risk, like when Mum and I made a beetroot and chocolate cake (which turned out to be AMAZING). Doing something new might end in disaster or it might turn out to be the best thing you've ever done – but if you never try, you'll never know.

"Do you think we're ready for tomorrow?" Mum had a smudge of dust on one cheek and her blonde hair was escaping from its ponytail.

"Yep," I said, looking around the new bakery. "I think we are."

Mum and I had been working together all afternoon preparing for the Sugar and

Spice Bakery's big opening. The glass counter and silver coffee machine gleamed. The wicker bread baskets were arranged in neat rows on wooden shelves. Five beautiful wedding and birthday cakes were displayed on silver stands next to a purple sofa with bright pink cushions, which stood beside a small, low table that had a brochure showing photographs of other cakes Mum had made on it. Along the front window of the bakery were four tall stools and there was a stack of pink-and-white paper bags by the till, each with the words *Sugar and Spice Bakery* printed across them in swirly letters.

At the moment, the big glass counter was empty, but tomorrow it would be filled with cupcakes decorated with buttercream icing, sugary doughnuts, cinnamon swirls and cheesy twists. Exactly as Mum and I had imagined it.

It was going to be awesome. Mum was going to do all the baking and a lady called Paula would serve the customers.

I was too young to be allowed to officially work in the shop, but Mum had said I could help out at the weekends and in the holidays. We'd make amazing cakes, melt-in-the-mouth pastries, all sorts of fresh bread. Mum was even going to offer her services making wedding and birthday cakes.

Mum put her arm around me. "If you'd told me a year ago that I would be standing here – in my very own bakery – I would never have believed you. So much has happened."

"It has been a totally crazy year," I agreed.

It really had. For most of my life, ever since Mum and Dad had divorced when I was two and Dad had moved to America, things had been pretty normal. Mum gave up training as a pastry chef and took a job at Nottingham University working as a receptionist with more sociable hours so she could look after me. I went to playgroup, then school, and in the holidays we'd bake and cook together. One of my first ever memories is of standing on a chair in our old kitchen wearing a huge apron, kneading soft, squishy dough with Mum, and then afterwards sitting on the sofa, eating the fresh, warm bread together. It's always been just Mum and me, you see – or at least it has until a year ago, when Mum met Mark.

It was love at first sight, Mum said. I hadn't minded. I liked Mark straightaway. He reminded me of a freshly baked granary loaf – strong, reliable and good for you. I was glad to see Mum so happy too, because I knew she got lonely sometimes. Best of all, when Mark tried the cakes and pastries Mum made, he encouraged her to do something we'd always talked about but never dared to do – set up her own bakery. He even looked after me and his four-year-old twins, Molly and Ella, while she went to college to learn about running a business.

After that, it all happened really quickly. Mum found a shop she could convert into a bakery in a little town called Ashingham, which is about an hour away from Nottingham. Just a week ago, at the start of the Easter holidays, Mum and Mark got married and we all moved to the new house and the bakery finally became ours.

And now, tomorrow, we finally open! Mark is starting his new job as a website developer, and the twins will go to their new childminder. Then, the week after that, I'll start at King William's, my new school.

My tummy flips over whenever
I think about it. It's hard enough
starting any new school halfway
through Year Six but, in Ashingham, if
you're in Year Six you don't go to a normal
primary school, you go to something called
a middle school. It's like a secondary school
but it only takes Years Six, Seven, Eight
and Nine. It'll mean that instead of being at
the top of the school – like I was at my old
primary school – I'll be almost the youngest
and at the bottom.

Mum and I went to have a look around. It's
really big and I'm sure I'm going to get lost.
In my old school there were seven classes in
the whole school; at King William's there are
five classes just in Year Six.

The good thing about changing schools is
that Mum has finally said I can have a mobile
phone, because I'll be walking to and from
school on my own. My best friends from my
old school, Lucy and Issy, have had mobiles
since September, but Mum said I had to wait
until my birthday in August. Now she's had

8

to give in. It's brilliant being able to text and phone people – not that I have any friends in Ashingham to text yet, but I hope I will soon.

"Earth to Hannah," Mum nudged me. "What are you thinking about?"

I shrugged. "Nothing."

She raised her eyebrows. She always knows when I'm not telling her the truth.

"Just school," I admitted.

Mum smiled. "You'll be fine. You've never had a problem making friends."

Easy for Mum to say. She isn't the one who has to do it. And even if she's right and I *do* make friends, it won't be like having Lucy and Issy – friends I've known since playgroup, who know everything about me. I hate not living just around the corner from them any more. We've been texting, phoning and emailing each other, but it's not the same.

Mum gave me a hug. "You'll be OK, I promise. I'm really proud of you, sweetie. You've coped with all these changes in a really grown-up way. And you've been so helpful. You're the best daughter in the world."

I forced my thoughts of Lucy and Issy away. "And you're the best mum in the world," I told her. "And the Sugar and Spice Bakery—" I gestured with my arm before she could get too soppy, "is going to be the best bakery in the world! Just wait and see. Soon, we'll have people queuing up for cupcakes."

Mum smiled. "Yep, and there'll be waiting lists for the Danish pastries . . ."

"Fighting over the doughnuts," I added.

"And everyone in the county will order their wedding and birthday cakes here," Mum finished.

We sighed happily and grinned at one another.

Just then, there was a knock at the door. Mark was outside, his dark curly hair looking messy as usual. He was smiling and trying to wave, but he had Molly holding one hand and Ella holding the other. The twins pressed their noses against the glass. Ella was dressed as Scooby Doo and Molly as a princess.

"Looks like we have company." Mum went to let them in.

I felt a flicker of disappointment. I'd enjoyed being alone with Mum today. Over the past few months, we haven't had much time together at all. Actually, that's an understatement. We've had NO time together. I'm hoping that will change, once everything has settled down. I mean, I know I'm lucky to have a stepfamily I like. Some people hate their stepbrothers and sisters, but Molly and Ella are really cute most of the time. I just wish they weren't quite so loud. They're always talking and arguing, asking questions and wanting drinks or stories. Especially from me. Mark says it's because they love having a big sister and they talk about me all the time. I don't mind really, but it makes our home a very noisy place. Much noisier than it used to be.

Ella has dark curly hair like Mark, and Molly's is long, straight and brown. They've both got brown eyes, but Ella's are dark, sort of like plain chocolate, and Molly's are more hazelnutty. Even if they were identical, though, you could never mix them up. Ella's a tomboy who loves dogs and pirates, whereas Molly loves princesses and anything pink and sparkly. If Ella was a cake she would be a chocolate brownie – easy to like and gooey on the inside; while Molly would be a pink meringue – girly and very sweet.

Molly twirled in front of me.

"Which princess am I?" she demanded.

I looked at her long pink dress and plastic tiara. "Rapunzel?"

Molly burst out laughing as if I'd said something completely stupid. "No, silly. I'm Aurora!" She ran to Ella. "Hannah doesn't know the difference between Aurora and Rapunzel!"

They both giggled.

"Who am I, then?" said Ella.

That was easy. "Scooby Doo."

She rolled her eyes. "Noooo! I've got a cloak on. See!" She showed me her red cloak.

"OK . . . so, what does that mean?"

"That I'm Super Dog, of course!"

"We've decided that when we grow up, I'm going to be a princess fairy gymnast," announced Molly. "And Ella's going to be Super Dog."

"Super Dogggggggg!" cried Ella, flinging her arms out and racing around the bakery. Molly followed her.

I gasped as they ran dangerously close to the five-tiered wedding cake decorated with pale pink sugar roses, which had taken Mum and me an hour to get into place. It wobbled alarmingly on its stand.

"No running around in the bakery, girls!" Mark said quickly.

"Girls, stop! Please!" Mum said. But the twins didn't.

"Last one to touch the door's a fat old donkey!" I yelled.

It was like magic. Molly and Ella both raced to the door.

"I got here first."

"No, I did."

It might not be quiet, but at least they were standing still. I felt a surge of pride. I was getting good at twin control.

"Thanks, Hannah," said Mum, giving me a grateful smile.

"I'll take them home," Mark said.

"We'll come too," said Mum. "We're about finished here and I'll be back early enough tomorrow." From now on, Mum's working days will start at half past four in the morning. That's when she'll have to go to the bakery and start making the bread and breakfast pastries in time for (what will hopefully be) the morning rush.

We herded the twins out of the bakery. Mum shut the door and locked it. "See you tomorrow," she told the shop.

"For the Sugar and Spice's Bakery very first day," I said.

Then Mum took my arm, we smiled at each other and set off for our new home.

POSSIBLE BIRTHDAY CAKES FOR THE TWINS

MOLLY'S **PRINCESS** CAKE!

Ice cream cone towers

Piped vines with fondant leaves

Lemon sponge castle

Green coconut grass

Blueberry jam moat

ELLA'S **SUPER DOG** CAKE!

White choc button eyes

chocolate sponge cake

Rice paper medallion

SD

Liquorice cape & mask

MY TIPS FOR USING FONDANT ICING:

1. Lightly ice the cake with pale buttercream icing first so that the cake sides will be smooth before you put the fondant icing on.

icing spatula

2. Dust the surface you're going to roll out the fondant icing on with icing sugar first.

3. Roll out the fondant icing using a silicone rolling pin - the icing won't stick as much as to a wooden rolling pin.

silicone rolling pin

2

WHUMPH!

I yelled in shock as something – or someone – landed square on my tummy, waking me from a dream where I was decorating ten different cakes all at once in front of a TV audience.

"Hannah!" Molly squealed. "Wake up!"

I'd barely sat up in bed when – WHUMPH! – Ella joined her.

"It's morning, Hannah!" she sang, throwing her arms around my neck. I think she was trying to hug me but it felt more like being strangled.

"It really *is* morning." Molly bounced off the bed and tugged open the curtains.

"Look!"

"Get up! Pleeeease," Ella begged.

I glanced at my alarm clock. Six o'clock. Instead of groaning as I normally would have done at that time in the morning, my heart jumped. Today was opening day! Mum would already be at the bakery. Right now she'd probably be taking the pastries out of the oven, and starting on the scones. In a few hours, the first customers would start hurrying in. I'd wanted to go with her first thing, but she'd said I deserved a lie-in after all the work we'd done yesterday, and had arranged for Mark to drop me off when he took the twins to their new childminder. I couldn't wait.

The twins were exploring my room now. One of the good things about moving was planning what my bedroom would look like. In our old flat, my room had been the same since I was six – pink curtains, fairies on the wall and a castle-shaped mirror – which is fine if you're six, but not so good when you're nearly eleven.

OK, so I didn't get the TV and laptop, but I do have pretty much everything else. I spent ages unpacking and getting it just right.

The twins pulled a drawer out from my desk.

"Nail varnish!" shouted Molly.

"Let's paint our nails!" Ella said, starting to unscrew the top of a silver polish.

I flung the duvet back and jumped up. "Oh, no!"

19

"Pleeeeeease," Molly wheedled.

"We like painting our nails," said Ella, looking at me with big brown eyes.

I'm sure they do, but I could imagine the mess they would make. No way was that happening in my perfect new room, no matter how good a big sister I was trying to be. "How about we go downstairs and make some pancakes instead?" I said, thinking quickly. "We've got everything we need – flour, eggs . . ."

"Pancakes! Yippee!" they both cried and ran to the door.

I pulled on my dressing gown and followed them.

"Is that you, Hannah?" Mark called sleepily as I padded along the landing in my slippers.

"Yeah. I've said I'll go down and make some pancakes with the twins."

"Do you need a hand?"

"No, don't worry. I'll be fine. I'll yell if I need you."

"Thanks," he said. "You're a star."

By the time I got to the kitchen the twins had already fetched the box of eggs.

"How do you crack an egg, Hannah?" Molly said, waving an egg over the table.

"Carefully!" I gasped, swooping before she could drop it. "First, we need a bowl." I got everything else out and then showed Molly how to crack the eggs against the side of the bowl and gently pull the two halves apart.

"You can do another two eggs like that, Molly, while Ella measures out the flour with me."

The twins did everything I asked, quiet for once as they concentrated hard. When the batter was ready, Molly and Ella dragged chairs over to where they could see the cooker and stood on them to watch what I was doing. I heated oil in the frying pan, then swirled a ladle of the batter around so it coated the base of the pan. I love making pancakes. OK, it's not strictly baking, but

21

there's something magical about watching the runny pale batter turn into a delicious golden pancake.

MY TIPS FOR MAKING PANCAKES:

1. Use a non-stick frying pan with fairly flat sides so you can toss it, and make sure it's not too heavy or you won't be able to toss the pancake easily.

2. Don't put too much batter in the frying pan or the pancake will be thick and rubbery.

3. Don't use too much butter to cook the pancake, just enough to coat the bottom of the pan.

"Yummy!" said Ella.

"Can I lick the bowl when we've finished?" Molly asked.

"It's not like cake mixture," I warned. "It won't taste nice."

"You just want it all for yourself," Molly said, pouting.

I grinned. "Oh, do I?" I remembered when
I was little and had made the same mistake
myself. I handed them a spoonful of batter
mixture.

"Go on, then. Try it," I invited, waiting for
their reaction.

"Yuck!" They pulled faces.

"Told you," I said, laughing. "Right,
it's time to toss the pancake!"

The twins whooped as I
flipped the pancake in the air
and caught it. Success!

Molly and Ella ate four
pancakes each – covered
with lemon and sugar. As
they ate I told them a story
about a magic pancake that could grant
wishes. It reminded me of Mum doing the
same thing with me, and it was pretty cool
being able to do it with my new little sisters.
Kind of how I'd always imagined being a big
sister would be. I suddenly felt really glad
that Mum had married Mark. Even if it did
mean that I had to put up with two human

alarm clocks waking me up every morning.

When the twins ran off to watch cartoons, I sat down to have two pancakes myself. Mark came downstairs and I offered him some too.

"Yes please, I never turn pancakes down." I poured the last of the batter into the pan. "Thanks for looking after the girls, Hannah." He looked around and grinned. "Even if the kitchen does look like a bomb's hit it!"

"Sorry," I said, glancing around at the dirty mixing bowls, the eggshells on the counter, the flour spilled on the table. I'd been so busy keeping an eye on the twins, I hadn't had time to tidy as I went.

"Don't worry, I'll clean up later," Mark said. "It was lovely of you to get up with them. Pity you have to start school next week really."

My stomach flipped like the pancake I'd just tossed. I didn't want to think about school yet. "I wonder how Mum's getting on?" I said. I'd texted her, but she hadn't replied.

"We'll soon find out." Mark glanced at the clock. "We should get a move on. Molly! Ella! Time to get dressed!"

I went upstairs to my room and opened my wardrobe. What to wear for opening day? I wanted something that I could help behind the counter in, something comfy but not scruffy. I decided on my new jeans and favourite blue t-shirt with a cupcake on the front. I added a navy hoody and trainers. Finally, I brushed my blonde hair and put it up into a ponytail. I checked my reflection. Yep, that would do. The Sugar and Spice Bakery, here I come!

OUR NEW HOUSE

Molly & Ella's room

Mark & Mum →

← my room

lounge →

3

"I'm going to wait by the car!" I called to Mark.

Outside, it was a beautiful spring day – the sun was shining and daffodils were dancing in the breeze. I spotted our new neighbour, Mrs Rees, standing near the front gate. She came to introduce herself the day we moved in, bringing her three little pug dogs to say hello. She's quite a large lady, in her late seventies (Mum thinks), and she has dyed, tightly-curled blonde hair. She's quite deaf, which means you have to talk loudly to her, but she seems very jolly. Mum says she has a grand-daughter the same age as me who also goes to King William's.

Today, Mrs Rees had only two of her pugs

with her. "Bobby! Come to Mummy!" she was calling. "Oh, Bobby, where are you? Bobb-eeeeee!"

"Are you OK, Mrs Rees?" I asked.

The two little pugs jumped up, wrapping their leads around Mrs Rees's legs and almost toppling her over. I grabbed her arm just in time and helped untangle her.

"Oh, thank you, Hannah dear!" she gasped. "I'm in a terrible pickle. I've gone and lost my little Bobby!"

Bobby? I was confused for a moment, before I remembered that was the third pug. "Oh, Bobby! Do you want me to help you look for him?"

"The brook!" Mrs Rees eyes widened in alarm. "You saw Bobby in the brook!"

"No!" I raised my voice. "I said, do you want me to help you LOOK?"

"Oh," said Mrs Rees. "Yes, please, dear. I'm sorry for the mix-up." She tapped her ear. "My hearing aid isn't working too well."

"Where did you last see Bobby, Mrs Rees?" I asked loudly.

"Well, I came out of the house with him and suddenly he wasn't there. He must have run off." She started to look around and call out. "Bobb-eeeeee! Bobbeeeee!"

I listened for a moment. I was sure I could hear a faint yapping and scrabbling sound. It seemed to be coming from Mrs Rees's house. I went down her driveway and, sure enough, the scrabbling was at the front door. "Mrs Rees! I think he's in your house. In there!" I pointed at the door.

Mrs Rees looked very puzzled. "You want to go in and brush your hair?"

"No." I had to stop myself from giggling now. I raised my voice to a shout. "I said I think Bobby's in THERE!"

"Really?" Mrs Rees looked surprised. "But how can he be?" She unlocked the door and a third little pug hurtled out. He jumped around Mrs Rees in delight, snuffling and yapping, his lead trailing on the ground.

"Oh, goodness gracious. I must have shut him inside!" she exclaimed. "How silly of me!"

I grabbed the lead and handed it to her.

"Here you are, Mrs Rees."

"Thank you, dear," said Mrs Rees. "That was very kind of you. So, how are you all settling in?"

"Fine, thanks!" I said, making sure I spoke as loudly as I could. "Mum's bakery opens today."

"Well, wish your mother luck from me. I shall try and pop in later and pick up a chocolate éclair for my tea."

"I could bring you one back if you want?" I offered.

"I'm just going to the bakery now." I was sure Mum wouldn't mind me giving away a chocolate éclair for free. And if Mrs Rees liked it, she might spread the word to her friends.

Mrs Rees beamed. "Oh, thank you, dear. Well, I'd best be off. My boys do like their walkies!" The three little dogs set off down the pavement, towing Mrs Rees along behind them.

I grinned. It looked to me as if the pugs

were taking Mrs Rees for a walk rather than the other way round.

I decided Mrs Rees would be a custard slice – layers of flaky pastry with custard oozing out – large, cheerful and welcoming.

Just then, Mark came out of the house with Molly and Ella. At last! We were ready to go.

The Sugar and Spice Bakery is in a small row of shops down a quiet street called Parson's Lane which joins on to the high street. Mum was a bit worried that people might not realise we're here, but in the end we decided it was pretty perfect and too good an opportunity to miss. The building is really lovely: it's old with a big bay window, much nicer than the modern shops in the main part of town. There are cherry trees outside, with branches full of fluffy blossom. Whenever I look at them I imagine cupcakes decorated with swirly pink icing.

As we pulled up outside, I jumped out of the car, waved to Mark and the twins, then pushed open the door of the bakery.

The bell tinkled welcomingly, and as I stepped inside I was hit by the delicious smell of fresh bread. The counters and shelves were filled with the cakes, pastries and bread Mum had spent the morning baking. The bottom shelf of the glass counter had three big cakes displayed that people could buy slices of – a carrot cake, a Victoria sponge and a chocolate cake – as well as a silver cake stand holding individual cupcakes, decorated with swirled frosting and delicate flowers. The top shelf was filled with croissants, Danish pastries and sausage rolls. The middle shelf was fairly empty, but I knew that was because Mum would still be baking the items that would go there – éclairs, scones, doughnuts, meringues – the teatime baked goods.

It looked even better than it had done yesterday and I smiled proudly. Strangely, though, apart from the woman behind the counter who was now staring at me, the shop itself was completely empty. Maybe it was stupid, but I'd sort of imagined that the second Mum opened the doors, there would be a stream of people desperate to sample her cakes.

The lady behind the counter was small and round, with short dark spiky black hair and brown eyes. Her black polo neck and jeans were covered by a large white apron. "Hello, love, can I help you?"

"Hi. I'm Hannah I . . . um . . . I'm looking for my mum."

"Hannah!" The lady's face lit up. "I should have guessed. You look just like your mum. I'm Paula." She wiped a hand on her apron and held it out to me.

"Pleased to meet you," I said.

Ah, so this was Paula, the lady who would be running the shop while Mum did the baking.

Paula smiled warmly. "I hear you're going to be helping out now and again, Hannah, so we'll be seeing a lot of each other. Right, let me guess . . ." She put her head on one side and studied me. "The wisdom and empathy of the water bearer or the zest for life and warm friendliness of the lion? Which is it?"

"Sorry?"

"Your star sign, silly!" Paula rolled her eyes, as if it should have been obvious. "When's your birthday?"

"Oh! It's 1st August."

"Then you're a Leo." Paula nodded. "I can always guess. I have a special talent for it. Well, you and I shall get along famously. I'm a Sagittarius and we get on very well with Leos."

I smiled. Paula must guess people's star signs like I decide what sort of cake or pastry people would be. Paula is definitely a scone fresh out of the oven – small, round, warm and friendly.

Just then, Mum poked her head through the door that led to the kitchen.

"Hannah! I thought I heard your voice." She was wearing white trousers and a white short-sleeved top, white clogs, a white hat and a white apron. She had a flour smudge on her nose and her cheeks were flushed.

"How's it all going?" I asked.

"Busy," she said. "I've been flat-out baking all morning. Though we've only had a couple of customers in so far, which is a bit worrying."

"I'm sure more people will come in soon," I said. "You've only been open a little while."

She smiled, though she still looked worried. "Yes, you're right, it'll all be fine." She went back into the kitchen and I followed her.

It was very hot in there. It wasn't a big room and every bit of space had been used up. There were three ovens, on top of each other, which were are all different temperatures for cooking different things – the top oven was the hottest and that was for the bread, the lower two ovens were cooler and were for the pastries and cakes. There was a stacking trolley with shelves for putting the loaves on before they went into the oven, and another trolley for the loaves when they came out.

There was a long baker's bench where Mum kneaded dough and rolled out pastry, cupboards for keeping the ingredients in, two large flour bins on coasters, and shelves that held a variety of black cast-iron loaf tins. I felt a thrill run through me. It was small, but it was all perfectly organised, with everything a baker could possibly need.

IMPORTANT THINGS TO REMEMBER

WHEN I OPEN MY OWN BAKERY

1. Always label the flour bins properly or you might end up mixing up the pastry flour and bread flour.

2. Never wash cast iron loaf tins, they 'season' and get better the more they are used.

3. Keep a brush to sweep the baker's bench surface instead of a cloth.

4. Wear something cool. It's VERY hot!

Mum pulled a tray of scones out of one of the ovens. They had risen beautifully, and raisins and sultanas peeped through a pale golden crust.

"Yum!" I said. "You *have* been busy."

"While these cool, I'd better finish the chocolate éclairs," she said. "We'll need those for the teatime rush."

We both glanced towards the empty shop and I knew we were thinking the same thing: if there *was* a teatime rush.

I remembered Mrs Rees and told Mum about taking her a chocolate éclair. Mum said that was fine. "I'll box one up for her as soon as they're ready."

"Do you want me to do anything?" I asked hopefully.

"Not just now, thanks." Mum looked stressed as one of the other ovens started to beep. "I've got to get the cheese scones out," she muttered, half to herself. "And the gingerbread men in."

"Are you sure I can't help?"

"I'm sorry, love. I need some space to

think right now. Can you help Paula in the shop instead?"

I felt a stab of disappointment. I'd hoped I'd actually get to *do* some of the baking today. "Oh. OK," I said.

"It's just for today," Mum said, seeing my face. "I really need to concentrate."

I nodded. "Sure." And I went back into the main shop, leaving the warm kitchen behind.

4

Paula was polishing the countertop.

"Can I do anything?" I asked.

"Not really, love. It's very quiet."

"Oh." What was I supposed to do all day? Hang around like a spare part?

Paula straightened up. "On second thoughts, I'm sure I can find you something to do," she said. "Your mum wants us to put some samples out for people to try when they come in. Maybe you could sort that out for me?"

"Sure," I said. I'd rather have been baking, but helping Paula was better than standing around doing nothing.

I washed my hands and set to work, cutting

slices of cake and chopping them into neat pieces, then putting them in bowls and labelling them. Meanwhile, Paula put the fresh scones in the counter and checked the levels of the coffee machine. We weren't a café, but Mum had wanted people to be able to buy a cup of tea or coffee to take away with them to drink with their purchases. She always said warm pastries tasted better with a hot drink.

As Paula and I worked, we chatted. Paula told me she had three grown-up children. She asked me what music I liked. I'm not really that into music, I told her. I just listen to whatever's in the charts. I'm not the sort of person to stick up posters of bands on my bedroom walls. I'd rather have posters of cakes! Paula loves music. And dancing. She told me her newest hobby was belly dancing. I must have stared. She's too old and . . . well, too *round* for belly dancing, surely?

"Honestly!" she insisted. "Watch this." Holding her hands above her head, she began to shimmy across the floor. It was the funniest thing I'd ever seen. Paula's quite short and, with her apron billowing out around her, she looked a bit like a tellytubby trying to belly dance. "Be-dum. Be-dum," she hummed. "Be-dummy-dummy-dum."

I couldn't help it. I laughed out loud. I clapped my hand over my mouth. "I'm sorry!"

For a moment, I thought Paula would be really cross, but her eyes twinkled. "I know, I know. I admit it, I look ridiculous," she said, chuckling. "Still, it keeps me fit and I love it. And at the moment I've a real reason for doing it. On Sunday we're doing a sponsored six-hour dance at the church hall to raise money for my nephew, Tom. He's really ill. He needs an operation in America but that's going to cost a lot of money. So . . ."  – she wiggled her hips some more – "we're dancing to try and raise some for him."

Paula was smiling but I felt a bit awkward. How awful to have a nephew who was so ill. "How old is your nephew?" I asked her.

"Eight."

Eight! Wow. That was four years younger than me. I'd seen children who were seriously ill on the news before. I'd never met anyone who had to live with that sort of thing on a daily basis.

"I'll sponsor you too," I said quickly.

"Thanks." She smiled. "The dance is going to be brilliant and raise lots of money. I know, because it says so in the stars. Look." She reached behind the counter and pulled out a magazine which was open at the horoscopes page. She pointed at Sagittarius.

"'A golden opportunity is dancing your way this weekend'," she read. "'Seize it with both hands and rags will turn to riches.' See? The stars are always right. And it says here that today Leos should remember that 'the golden key of kindness can open any door'."

"What does that mean?" I asked.

Paula tapped her nose. "I'm sure all will be revealed."

"OK," I said. I didn't really believe in horoscopes, but I didn't want to offend Paula and, anyway, I really hoped this horoscope would come true and her dancing would be a success.

The shop door opened and a girl came in. She had shoulder-length strawberry blonde hair and a scattering of freckles across her nose and cheeks. My heart leaped. Our first customer – and it was someone the same age as me.

"Hi," I said eagerly.

The girl walked straight to the counter, ignoring me completely.

I felt a rush of disappointment.

"Hello, love. What can I get for you?" Paula said.

"Two sausage rolls, please," the girl said. As Paula started to get the sausage rolls out, the girl spotted the bowls with the cake samples. "Could . . . could I try a piece of cake, please?"

43

"Help yourself," said Paula.

The girl took a piece of the Victoria sponge. I expected her to just eat it quickly but she chewed it carefully. "Wow. This is really light," she said, looking at Paula. "But it's rich too. Was it made with butter or margarine?"

I blinked. I'd never met anyone my age who would even think to ask a question like that. Lucy and Issy definitely wouldn't, and they'd heard me going on about baking for most of our lives.

"I don't know, love," said Paula. "Let me check."

"Actually, it's half and half," I said, going over. "I'm Hannah. My mum owns the bakery. Try the chocolate and beetroot cake too – it's amazing."

The girl took a piece. "Wow! There's something else unusual in this, isn't there? Is it sour cream?"

I was surprised. "Yes! How did you know?"

44

She shrugged. "I've tried adding sour cream to chocolate cakes before, but I've never added beetroot."

I could have somersaulted in delight. Here was someone who seemed to like baking almost as much as I did. I wondered if she went to King William's.

Paula handed her the wrapped up sausage rolls.

"Here you are, love. That'll be £2.50, please.'

The girl handed over the money and headed for the door.

"Hang on a sec," I said. I wanted her to stay; I wanted to get to know her, to talk more about baking. "What's your name?"

She stopped by the door. "I'm Mia." But before I could ask any more she slipped out, the door shutting behind her. I stared after her, frustrated. Great. Project 'Making Friends' was off to a fantastic start. Not.

I spent the rest of the morning hoping that someone else my age would come in. I couldn't understand how I seemed to have blown it with Mia and why she hadn't stayed to chat. Nobody my age did come in, though. In fact, there were hardly any customers at all.

"It's not very busy, is it? Is there another bakery in town?" I asked Paula as we stood at the counter.

Paula shook her head. "Not really. Just the supermarket. We are a bit tucked away down this street, though. People don't really just happen to walk past. What advertising has your mum done?"

"Not much," I said. "She's put some adverts in the local paper and Mark's designed a website for the bakery. I know she was going to print some leaflets and have them delivered to people's houses, but things have been so busy, I don't think she's had time."

"It's a shame," said Paula. "Ashingham needs a local business like this. Still, I'm sure once people hear about it and come and taste your mum's cakes, they'll soon tell all their friends."

I looked at her thoughtfully, an idea

forming in my head. Maybe if people tasted the food they would start coming in. "I could stand outside and offer people samples as they walk by," I suggested.

Paula smiled. "Great minds think alike! I thought the very same thing this morning. I tried standing outside with a plate of cut-up croissants and Danish pastries but almost no one came by to taste them. It's just not a busy enough street."

Hmm. There had to be *something* we could do to get more customers in. As I looked around at the empty shop and the full shelves and baskets my heart sank – the Sugar and Spice Bakery's first day wasn't turning out how I'd imagined at all.

5

The bakery continued to be quiet. There were busy moments when people from some of the offices and shops on the street came in, and we had a few passing customers, but there were also long periods of time when the shop was empty.

At three o'clock, I poked my head into the kitchen. "When are we going home, Mum?"

"I'm going to stay open till half past four, just to see if there's a late afternoon rush," said Mum. "But you walk home if you want. You've got your key and your phone so you can ring me if you need anything. Remember all the usual rules, though."

"Yes, don't open the door to strangers.

Don't use the oven without you or Mark there. Get out of the house if there's a fire," I recited.

"And go next door to Mrs Rees in an emergency," said Mum.

I nodded. "Shall I take her éclair with me? I could drop it off on the way home."

"Good idea. You can take her a couple. It's not as if we haven't got plenty left." Mum sighed. "See you later, sweetie."

I set off for home. Poor Mum. She'd been working so hard, but we'd hardly sold anything. Some of the cakes could be put in tins and stored until the next day, but the pastries, bread and cream cakes wouldn't keep.

I shook my head, trying to clear the depressing thoughts. Thinking like that wasn't going to help. What I should be doing was working out how we could get more customers.

I stopped at Mrs Rees's house to drop the éclairs off first. At least someone would get to enjoy Mum's baking today. She was delighted. "Thank you so much, my dear. And extra ones too," she said, looking inside the box.

"That's very kind of you and your mum. You really must meet my grand-daughter, Alice. She's the same age as you and goes to King William's. I'm sure you'd get on famously."

I smiled. I always think it's weird how adults think you'll get on with someone just because you're the same age. They don't like everyone who's the same age as them, do they? Still, it would definitely be good to know at least one person in my year, I supposed, even if she *was* forced into being nice to me by her grandma.

I said goodbye to Mrs Rees and let myself into the house. I was used to it being full of the twins and Mum and Mark, and it seemed very quiet without them. Back in our old flat, I used to quite enjoy it when Mum left me on my own for a little while. And if for some reason I didn't want to be alone, I could always call round for Lucy or Issy. Their houses were like second homes to me. I felt a pang of loneliness. Even if I did meet new people in Ashingham, I wasn't sure if there would ever be anyone I'd feel so comfortable with as I did with my oldest friends.

I felt a sudden surge of homesickness. I pulled out my phone to call Lucy, but her mobile went straight to voicemail. So did Issy's.

I knew it was silly of me to be upset, but I couldn't help it. I had to find something to do instead of moping. That's what Mum always tells me when she catches me feeling sorry for myself. (Though she usually suggests something boring like emptying the dishwasher or taking the bins out.) I remembered again what Paula had said about advertising. Fetching my journal, I started to write down some ideas.

HOW TO GET MORE CUSTOMERS

- Give out samples of cake. WHERE?
- Make advertising leaflet - pictures of cakes? Biscuits? Opening hours?
- Voucher in leaflet for free cup of coffee?
- Find places to give out leaflet. INTERNET?

I went to the computer and typed Ashingham into the search engine. The first thing that came up was a tourist information website. Exactly what I needed. Even better, the first item that was posted under "Things to Do" was the farmers' market, which took place on the third Saturday of every month in the town centre. The next one was this weekend.

My mind started whirring. We could go there and give out cake samples and leaflets! It was bound to be really busy and once people tasted Mum's amazing baking, they would be queuing out of the door to buy her cakes and pastries: they'd travel from nearby villages; she might be on local news. Well, maybe I was getting a bit ahead of myself, but it would be a start, at least.

I spent the rest of the afternoon designing a leaflet, and when I heard Mum's key in the door, it was five o'clock. I ran downstairs. I couldn't wait to tell her my idea.

Mum came in and plonked three huge bags of pastries and bread on the floor. She looked exhausted. "Are you OK?" I asked.

She smiled wearily. "Yes. Just completely whacked. It's been a long day. And I can't help feeling it was a waste of time." She glanced at the bags at her feet. "I gave Paula the rest of the leftovers. She's going to give them to her friends and family." She gave a sad laugh. "I never thought I'd have to give away everything I baked on the first day."

"Things will get better, I know they will," I told her. "I've started designing a leaflet and—"

"Whoa, Hannah!" Mum held up her hands. "I'm sure your ideas are great, sweetheart. I just need five minutes to sit down and have a cup of tea and think about dinner. Unless you want Danish pastries and doughnuts?"

"Oh. OK."

Mum forced another smile. "I'm sorry. Look, let me sit down for a few minutes, then you can tell me everything."

"Sure." I went into the kitchen and put the kettle on.

Mum sat at the big table, rubbing her

forehead. When I handed her a cup of tea, she wrapped her hands around it and let out a sigh.

"This is exactly what I needed. We might not have had many customers but I've still hardly had a chance to sit down all day." She shook her head. "Although one good thing happened. Just as I was closing up, a lady came in to ask if I'd make a dinosaur birthday cake for her son."

"That's great!" I said. "I can help you design it, like we did for Issy last year! We can do it after you've had your cup of tea."

Mum started to look a bit brighter. "That would be brilliant. She's coming back the day after tomorrow. I said I'd have a couple of designs for her to look at."

I was already starting to see dinosaur cakes in my head. "It could be a landscape with little dinosaur models made out of fondant icing dotted around it or it could be a cake in the shape of a dinosaur or—"

Just then, the front door opened and the sound of people and noise filtered in from the hallway. It was Ella, Molly and Mark.

"Can I have something to eat?" Molly said, shrugging out of her coat and trainers and leaving them on the floor.

"Can I put the TV on?" said Ella, throwing off her coat and shoes too. "What's for dinner?"

"A cup of tea! That looks good!" said Mark. "Who wants another?"

Mum and I looked at each other. I could tell what she was thinking, because I was thinking it too. One minute it had been just the two of us, chatting quietly together, and now . . . well, now it was very different.

"Can we have pasta for tea?" asked Molly.

"No, I want pizza," said Ella. "Pizza and olives."

"Olives are yucky," said Molly. "They taste like rabbit poo."

"You don't know what rabbit poo tastes like," said Ella.

"I do, and it tastes like olives! I want

pasta and cheese." Molly looked at Mum. "Pleeeeeaase."

"I want pizza!" Ella's eyes filled with tears.

Mum groaned. "I'll do pizza *and* pasta. Why don't you both go and watch TV for a while?"

Mark gave Mum a quick kiss and then started to pick up the girls' clothes and empty their lunchboxes. "So how was the big first day?"

"Tiring," Mum said. She started to tell him all about it. I slipped out of the kitchen. It looked as though we weren't going to be doing the cake design or talking about my leaflet now. I went upstairs trying not to feel too hurt, but I couldn't stop myself shutting my bedroom door with more of a bang than was strictly necessary.

6

When I arrived at the bakery next morning, Paula was busy filling the bottom shelf of the counter with cakes. "Hi, love."

"Hi," I said, but my spirits sank as I looked around. The shop was just as beautiful as it had been yesterday, but there wasn't a single customer.

Mum came out from the back. She looked slightly less frazzled today, so at least that was good. "Hannah. Just in time! Come and try some of this sourdough."

Mmm. I love sourdough! I followed her into the kitchen. The air was heavy with the smell of freshly baked bread. There were four loaves on the workbench. They had crusty

tops dusted with a light coating of flour.
Mum had cut a slice from one. She put some
butter on, then handed it to me. I took a huge
mouthful.

"Well?" Mum said.

"Oh, wow!" I said. "Mmm."
Mum's sourdough is the
best – the inside is chewy and
soft, the outside crust has just the
right amount of crunch and a slightly sweet
flavour. It really is amazing.

"It's awesome!" I said.

Mum looked pleased. "If we can get
everyone in Ashingham feeling the same
way as you do about my baking, we'll be
OK!"

"It's strange that the thing that makes it
taste so good smells so gross," I said.

"What? You mean this? The starter?" Mum
picked up a glass jar from the table. It was
filled with a beige sludge. She took the lid off
and pushed it under my nose.

I immediately recoiled. "Ew! Yes, that!"
Most bread is made with yeast, to make it

rise, but sourdough is made with a special sourdough starter instead. The beige sludge has a strong vinegary smell, almost like something going bad.

SOURDOUGH STARTER

- Makes delicious bread - also crumpets and pizza bases.
- When you cook with it, you take what you need from the jar, then add more flour and warm water to what is left and stir it well. So you never use it up completely, you just keep adding to it.
- Some bakeries have sourdough starters that can be years and years old!

Mum shut the lid and tilted the mixture so it ran gloopily up the sides of the jar.

"It's a bit like batter," I realised, thinking

about the pancakes Molly, Ella and I had made yesterday.

Mum blinked. "What do you mean?"

"Well, batter tastes horrible raw, like this, but when you cook it, it tastes amazing. Just like when you bake the sourdough."

Mum considered for a moment. "Yes, I suppose that's true. Now, I just need some customers to come in and buy it!" She was smiling but I could see the worry lines between her eyes deepen as she glanced at the empty shop.

I decided now might be a good time to tell her my idea about the leaflet. "I'll show you the design tonight when we get home," I finished.

"It's a really good idea," she said. "I know I should have done more about the advertising but I was so busy with the wedding and the move and the baking that I ran out of time. Thanks, sweetie. Right, now," she adjusted the hat on her head, "I'd really better get on. Can you go out to the front and help Paula?"

"Can't I help you in here?" I said.

"Not today. Maybe tomorrow."

"But you said that yesterday," I protested.

"I'm sorry, darling – I need to work out what my routine is going to be on a normal working day and I can't do that if I'm chatting to you or explaining things. Can you take those loaves through?"

I shrugged. "I guess."

Mum sighed. "I'm sorry, Hannah, OK? It won't always be like this, I promise."

I picked up the loaves and walked into the shop. Well, maybe it was more of a stomp. But as I carried the loaves to the baskets, the smell of the fresh bread wafted into my nostrils and I stopped feeling so cross. It's impossible to smell fresh bread and feel grumpy at the same time. If you don't believe me, try it!

Now I come to think of it, there are lots of things like sourdough. I suppose even chocolate doesn't taste nice when it's just cocoa beans. One of the magical things about baking is that you can take something that looks horrible and turn it into something delicious.

FOOD THAT DOESN'T SEEM NICE AT FIRST
BUT IS DELICIOUS WHEN IT'S COOKED

1. Sourdough bread
2. Pancakes
3. Yorkshire puddings
4. Choux pastry
5. Scrambled eggs

For the rest of the morning I helped Paula behind the counter. I told her about my leaflet and idea to go to the farmers' market.

"That sounds a great plan," she said.

The bell on the door tinkled and a teenage boy wearing glasses came in.

"Morning, Neil!" Paula greeted him. "You found us, then?" The boy had a rucksack on his back and his nose was buried in a book about birds. He looked up.

"Did you hear there's been a sighting of an Iberian chiffchaff in one of the gardens on Park Avenue?" His eyes gleamed. "An Iberian chiffchaff!" he repeated, as if he was announcing the Queen had come to visit. "I have to go to see it for myself!"

"Great," said Paula cheerfully. "What can I get for you?"

He gazed at the counter. "A cheesy twist, please," he said finally, before looking down at his book again.

He took the pastry, paid his money and hurried out.

Paula raised her eyebrows at me. "Bird-crazy, that boy. Always has been."

I didn't care. He was a customer – that was the important thing! Maybe he had other bird-crazy friends he could tell about the bakery.

Our next customer was a man called Dennis, who seemed determined to be gloomy whatever Paula said.

"Lovely day, isn't it?"

"It's too sunny. The ground needs rain," he replied.

"Oh well," she said. "I heard a good shower is forecast tonight."

"Huh!" Dennis said. "It'll be the wrong

sort of rain. Too much at once." He shook his head. "You mark my words."

"I will!" Paula smiled as she took his money and I handed him the wrapped-up loaf of bread and the strawberry tart he had just bought.

"Bye," I said. "Have a nice day!"

He glowered and walked out, shaking his head. Paula and I giggled. It was fun helping Paula, I decided. Not as much fun as baking, of course, but I was having a good time.

People continued to call in throughout the morning. Most of them were Paula's friends, but they were still paying customers, and I could tell Mum was relieved.

Just before midday, the shop door opened and Mrs Rees came in. With her was a girl about my age, who I assumed must be the grand-daughter she'd mentioned. The girl was tall, slim and really pretty, with long brown hair and hazel eyes. She smiled at me and I smiled back.

"Hello, Marion! Hello, Alice!" Paula said.

"Hi, Paula," said Mrs Rees. "Alice is

visiting today and we thought we'd call in and get something for lunch. Those chocolate éclairs I had yesterday were quite simply the best I've ever tasted."

She saw me and waved. "Ah, it's Hannah."

"Hi, Mrs Rees." I smiled again at Alice. "Hi," I said to her.

"Gran says you've just moved here and you're coming to King William's," she said.

I nodded. "Yes, I'm in Year Six."

"Me too. Do you know which form you're in?"

"6DC."

Alice's face lit up. "Same as me. Cool."

I felt suddenly hopeful. Alice seemed so nice, she would probably have loads of friends already. She wouldn't need some new girl hanging around. But at least she was being friendly, and it would be nice to have someone to say hello to when I started on Monday.

"What can I get for you?" Paula asked Mrs Rees. She seemed to know her well, and spoke loudly and clearly. "Another couple of éclairs, some iced buns maybe?"

Mrs Rees fanned herself. "I'm rather out of breath after the walk down here. Maybe I'll just sit down and have a cup of tea and then decide." She sank onto the sofa and Paula fetched her a cup of tea.

Alice came over to me. "You're really lucky having a mum who's a baker. You must have loads of nice things to eat."

"Hmm." I smiled. "Frozen pizza and more frozen pizza at the moment – unless I cook myself."

Alice looked puzzled.

I explained. "Since moving here, Mum's been so busy with the bakery that she hasn't had much time to cook at home." I paused, searching for something more to say. "Do . . . do you want to try some of the bread my mum's just made?" I cringed as the words came out. It was such a lame question. But Alice nodded.

"Yes please!"

We went to the kitchen. Mum was taking a tray of apple tarts out of the oven.

"Mum, this is Alice, Mrs Rees's granddaughter."

Mum smiled at Alice. "Hi, Alice. It's nice to meet you."

"Please can we have some of that leftover sourdough bread?" I asked.

"Of course," said Mum. "But then you'd better go back into the front of the shop. I've got some hot trays to move around."

I took a slice of bread for each of us and we left Mum to it.

"This is really nice," Alice said, nibbling at the sourdough.

I was about to tell her that that was because it's made with a sourdough starter instead of yeast, but I stopped myself just in time. Baking talk hadn't worked with Mia yesterday, and I didn't want Alice to run away like Mia had.

"So, have you seen much of the town yet?" Alice asked.

"Not really. We've been so busy getting the bakery up and running."

"Why don't I show you around a bit?"

I felt a rush of relief. She must think I seemed OK to make an offer like that. "Sure," I said happily. "Sounds great."

7

Mrs Rees and Mum said it was fine for
Alice and me to go out for a while. We set
off into the sunshine, heading towards the
town centre. As we walked, Alice asked lots
of questions and I asked lots back. I always
like finding out things about new people.
It's a bit like working out the ingredients
in a mystery cake – learning all the things
that go into making them the person they
are.

Alice told me that she loves horses and she
has an older sister called Rachel. She's lived
in Ashingham all her life. Her best friends
are called Misha and Lara and they're in form
6DC too.

MY NEW FRIEND ALICE

ALICE: pretty, nice, she'd be the sort of cake everyone likes; fun but cool too. A vanilla cupcake.

I told her about Lucy and Issy and how we usually spend the holidays – going to the swimming pool, the cinema, sometimes the park, sometimes baking at my house. It made me feel a bit sad to talk about them, but I tried not to show it. It was good to chat to someone my age instead of just being with Mum and Mark, or the twins. We swapped mobile numbers. I felt a buzz as I added her name to my contacts list. I finally had a friend in Ashingham! The more I talked to Alice, the more I felt that maybe we really *could* be friends. She seemed very like me – apart from the fact that she didn't like baking. That was OK. I could teach her about baking and she could teach me about horses! I wondered what Misha and Lara would be like. If they were anything like Alice, I was sure we'd get along.

"This is the town centre," said Alice, when we reached a small square with a statue in the middle of it. "The park's down that way. We go there quite a lot."

Ahead of us, I spotted a girl standing on the corner checking her phone. It was Mia. I nudged Alice and nodded in Mia's direction. "That girl came into the bakery yesterday. Do you know her?"

"Yeah. That's Mia Roberts. She's in our year too, but a different tutor group."

"Is she nice?" I asked.

Alice considered the question. "I'm not sure. Misha thinks she's stuck-up because she never speaks to anyone. I don't know, though. She never does anything horrible.

She just keeps herself to herself. Anyway, the park's this way." She walked on.

I hesitated for a moment. I wanted to go and say hi to Mia, but she hadn't seemed too keen to chat yesterday. Maybe Alice's friend was right and Mia *was* stuck-up. It's just that when we'd been talking about the chocolate and beetroot cake she had seemed OK . . .

"Come on!" Alice called over her shoulder. I hurried after her.

The park was much nicer than the rather scruffy park that had been close to our old house. This park had green railings and large expanses of neat grass, flowerbeds filled with daffodils and trees surrounded by crocuses. There was a play area and a fountain in the middle with low walls around to sit on. Near the fountain there was a toilet block and a small kiosk selling sweets and ice creams.

Alice and I sat on one of the walls. "There's a skate park over there," she said, pointing to the far side of the park. "And a duck pond that way with some very greedy ducks. They chased me once when I trying to feed them. I was only four – they were huge!" She pointed in another direction. "Me, Misha and Lara come here in the holidays, when we're not at the stables."

"Do you all ride?" I asked.

She nodded. "How about you?"

"No. I've been pony trekking a few times. The first time I was put on this tiny shaggy pony and all it wanted to do was eat. It put its head down to eat the grass and I fell off."

Alice giggled. "Little ponies can be really naughty. You should come for lessons. There's a beginners group on Saturdays. The ponies at our stables are really well behaved."

I smiled. "I think I'll just stick to watching." I was pleased she'd asked but, if things went to plan, Saturdays would be the busiest days at the bakery, and Mum would need my help.

I swung my legs and looked around the park. There were mums pushing buggies or sitting on benches watching their children play, boys playing football on the grass and people jogging and cycling. On the other side of the fountain there was a group of tough-looking girls who were about twelve. They were being loud and pushing each other about.

"They're in the year above us," said Alice, following my gaze.

I'd seen groups like that at my old school, picking on others, usually the quiet ones who didn't have many friends. I've never set out to be one of the popular ones, but people usually seem to want to be friends with me, and bullies tend to ignore me. I'm not stupid, though. I know it's best to not get noticed by them, especially when they're hanging around in a gang and looking bored.

Just then, a girl came out of the toilets behind us. She was tall and broad-shouldered. Her dark hair was spiked up and she was wearing a short skirt and black ankle boots with a sharp heel. Her face was hard, as if she was angry about something.

I caught my breath as she walked by – her

74

skirt was tucked into her knickers at the back.

"Look!" I hissed.

Alice's hands flew to her mouth. "How embarrassing is that?"

"We should tell her," I said.

"Are you kidding? That's Tegan McGarrity!" Alice looked horrified.

I was too busy watching the girl sauntering past us to take in the name. Not even the toughest person in the world can look scary with their skirt caught in their knickers. I remembered when I'd been in Year Four and had gone to the toilets at lunchtime and then walked back into the dining hall with *my* skirt tucked into my knickers. Everyone had burst out laughing and I'd wanted the floor to open up and swallow me. It was completely humiliating.

"We can't let her walk back to her mates like that," I said. "We've got to tell her."

Alice still didn't move so I jumped up. I know it was a bit mad but I just had to. I hate watching people being embarrassed.

"Hey!" I called after her. "Hey, you!" I
realised I couldn't remember what Alice had
said the girl's name was. It began with a T
and there had been an "r" sound in it, hadn't
there? I made a wild guess. "Tigger!" Even as
I shouted it, I knew it didn't sound right.

Alice gave a squeak like a terrified mouse.

The girl swung round. Even with the
distance between us I could see anger in her
dark eyes. Her face creased into a scowl.

"WHAT did you just call me?" She
marched slowly back towards us.

Oh help. Maybe it hadn't been a good idea
to call out. She seemed pretty annoyed. And
she seriously didn't look like someone you
wanted to annoy. "Sorry," I said. "I don't
know your name. It's just your skirt—"

"What about my skirt?" Her fists clenched
at her sides. Her face was close to mine now.
I took a deep breath.

"Your skirt. It's . . . caught in your pants."

The girl stopped. Her hand reached behind
her, but she kept looking at me suspiciously,
as if she thought I was winding her up. I saw

her feel where the material was caught in her knickers. An expression of horror crossed her face. She hastily pulled her skirt down.

"Sorry," I said again. "I just thought you'd want to know."

The girl glared at me. Then her shoulders relaxed and she stopped looking as if she wanted to push me into the duck pond. "Right. Thanks," she muttered.

"That's OK. I'm Hannah, by the way."

The girl gave me a nod. "Tegan."

I risked a grin. "Not Tigger, then?"

For a moment something that looked almost like a smile flickered back across Tegan's face. "Call me Tigger again and you'll be sorry," she growled. "Laters, Hannah." She turned and walked back to her friends.

Alice was staring at me, her face pale. "Did that just happen?" she said. "Did you really just call Tegan McGarrity 'Tigger' and tell her her skirt was caught in her pants – and *survive*?"

I frowned. "Yeah. I guess I did."

"No one in our year – and I mean NO

ONE – speaks to Tegan unless she speaks to them first, and usually when that happens it's very bad news." Alice mimed cutting her throat. "She got suspended last term for bullying and she's always in trouble. Misha was at primary school with her. Misha says Tegan was OK then but she's definitely not OK now."

"Oh." I glanced across to where Tegan was messing about with her friends, throwing Coke cans at one another. I suppose it had been a bit of a risk. Tegan actually hadn't been that bad; she'd seemed quite grateful, once she realised I was trying to help her.

Alice started to giggle. "I can't believe you just called Tegan McGarrity 'Tigger'! Wait till I tell Misha and Lara. Tigger!" She snorted with laughter.

I grinned, pleased at her reaction, though that wasn't why I'd done it.

Alice linked my arm. "I know Misha and Lara are going to really like you. We'll ask if you can sit with us when school starts. If you want to?"

Did I want to? I wanted to jump up and down like one of Mrs Rees's pugs and shout, "Yes, please! Yes please!", but instead I just gave her a smile. "Sounds good to me."

She smiled back and we set off towards the bakery.

8

"Looks like it's bread and cream cakes for tea tonight," Mum said, as she looked around the shelves that afternoon. It was three o'clock and there were still plenty of loaves of bread in the baskets and cream cakes in the glass counter. "We've had a few more people in, but still nowhere near enough."

"It will get better," I said. "It's only the first week." I had taken some photos on my phone of the pastries and loaves of bread. "I'll finish designing my leaflet tonight, then we can print them out and take them to the farmers' market on Saturday morning with some cake samples."

"Saturday?" said Mum. "But I'll need to be

here baking and Paula will be serving."

I hesitated. "Oh well, I suppose I can go on my own." I felt a bit nervous about the idea, but I'd do it for Mum.

Mum didn't look so sure. "You're not really old enough to go on your own. Mark's taking the twins over to their gran's first thing. He'll be back after that, though. I'll ask him if he can come with you."

"Great," I said. "Mark and I can do it together."

Mum smiled, her weariness lifting slightly. "You're really determined about this advertising, aren't you?"

I nodded. Going to the market was the perfect way to let more people know about us. "People are bound to come when they taste your cakes."

"Well, thank you. I really appreciate it," Mum yawned. "Oh dear, I'd better start cleaning up that kitchen now, though I'm aching all over."

"That's because you're trying to do it by yourself," said Paula, bustling in from the kitchen. "You need some extra help with all that baking. I told you about my friend Jane's son, didn't I? He's looking for the experience and he'd be perfect. You could take him on as an apprentice."

"Sorry, Paula," Mum said. "I'd love to but I can't afford to pay anyone else at the moment – even an apprentice. We're not making any money as it is."

"I'll go home now and finish the leaflet," I said. "That will help." It had to, I thought.

"Thanks, love. Mark will be back at half past five – ring if you need me. I'll be a bit later than normal. I had a phone call from a lady who has seen our website and wants to come in to talk about a fiftieth birthday cake."

"OK, well, I'll see you when I see you." I gave her a quick kiss and went to get my coat.

As soon as I got home, I sat down at the computer and got to work on the leaflet. I

tried to make the bakery sound
like a real family business. I
included the names of the
local mill where Mum got
her flour, and the farms that
supplied her with fruit and eggs
and milk. I remembered what Paula
had said about needing more local businesses
in Ashingham – I was sure people would
like to know that Mum was using local
ingredients. I added the photos I'd taken
on my phone and also included the opening
hours, telephone number and designed a
voucher for a free cup of coffee that people
could cut off the bottom. When I finally
pressed Save on the computer, I sat back
feeling tired but happy. I printed out a copy.
I hoped Mum would be pleased, and crossed
my fingers that my plan would work.

When Mark and the twins got home, I
shouted a quick hello, then went to my room
and shut the door. I didn't feel like dealing
with the usual demands for drinks and snacks
and stories.

I sat at my desk and doodled some more cake designs for the dinosaur cake. I could hear the TV on in the living room and Molly and Ella's voices raised in an argument, then Mark intervening. It felt strange sitting in my room, listening to the sounds of family life, as if I wasn't really part of it. In our old flat, I'd either have been hanging out with friends or baking with Mum at this time of day. I sighed.

From downstairs came the sound of Molly screaming and Ella starting to cry. Ugh – I know they're only little, but they're so annoying sometimes. I wished Mum would hurry up and come home.

It was after seven o'clock by the time Mum finally came through the door. I hurried to meet her. Molly and Ella beat me to it.

"Come and see my den!" cried Ella.

"Come and see my princess books," said Molly, pulling her hand. "I've put them all in order."

"Mum!" I said. "I've finished the bakery leaflet for Saturday." I waved it.

"Sorry, Hannah, I'll look at it later," Mum said. "Molly and Ella want to show me some stuff."

I blinked. What? This was a leaflet I'd done for *her*. She could at least *look* at it. "Mum, please."

"Later, Hannah. I've got to do this now." She turned away.

Something snapped inside me. "Oh, forget it! There'll probably be something else more important later too!"

"Hannah!" I heard the surprise in Mum's voice as I stomped upstairs. I didn't stop though. Why did I always have to be the one who waited? Why was I always the one Mum didn't have time for?

Throwing the leaflet on my desk, I sat down on my bed, so angry I could hardly breathe. Then, gradually, guilt started poking at me. Was I being unfair? Mum was trying to do so much. Setting up a new business, working in a new town. The twins were only four. Of course she had to give them attention first. But another smaller, meaner part of me couldn't help thinking that Mum wasn't the only one with a lot to deal with – I'd left my best friends behind, I was starting a new school, having to make new friends all over again, just so she could start her dream bakery. Why didn't she get that? She'd barely even asked me how I was feeling about everything, just told me I'd make friends easily and that was that. She could at least pretend to be interested.

A little while later, there was a knock at my door.

"Yeah?" I muttered.

"Hannah, it's me. Can I come in?"

Yes, please! Please come in, I thought. But I didn't say it. "If you want."

Mum came in and shut the door behind her. "I'm sorry," she said, standing awkwardly by my bed.

I stared at the floor. I wanted to be nice and say I was sorry too, but all my angry, bitter feelings were stopping the words coming out.

Mum sighed. "Look, I know you've been working hard on your leaflet and it's a brilliant idea, it really is. I'm very grateful. I shouldn't have asked you to wait." She sat on the bed next to me and put her arm around me. I stiffened and edged away.

"Hannah, please, don't be like this," she said. "I need you to be sensible and understanding."

I heard the unhappiness in her voice. I knew she was trying. Making a superhuman effort, I let go of the breath I was holding. *Be nice, be nice,* I told myself. Mum's having a hard time.

"I just wanted to show you what I'd been doing," I mumbled.

"I know," she said. "And I'm really sorry."

She did look genuinely sorry. I sighed, the horrible feelings retreating slightly. "OK. I'm sorry too." Mum budged up beside me and put her arm around me. This time I didn't move away.

"I know it must seem as if I don't have much time for you right now, but things will get easier," she said. "While things are settling down I just need you to be as grown-up as you can be. The twins are too little to realise that I'm busy and stressed, but I know you're old enough to understand how important this bakery is and why I need to put all my energy into it."

I shut my eyes. *I don't want to be understanding,* I shouted in my head. *I don't want to be a grown-up. I want my mum back.*

"Is that OK?" she went on. "Can you try really hard?"

I licked my lips. They were dry. "Yep. 'Course I can. I have been."

"I know." Mum squeezed my shoulders. She smiled, as if a weight had suddenly been lifted. "You're amazing, Hannah. I always know I can count on you. Now how about we look at this leaflet? Where is it?"

I went to my desk, my throat felt tight from holding back all the words I wanted to say but couldn't because Mum was counting on me. Returning with the leaflet, I handed it over. "Here."

Mum read it.
"Goodness, this is
great, Hannah!" she
said. "These photos
look fantastic and you've
got just the right amount
of information, and the idea
for a free coffee is fab. You really did this all
yourself?"

I nodded.

"I'm really impressed, sweetie. I'll definitely
use it. I'll get Mark to print copies at work
and you can take them to the farmers' market
on Saturday morning. Now, shall we have a
think about this dinosaur cake design?"

I looked at her in surprise. "What about the
twins? Won't they need you to make supper
and give them a bath?"

"No, it's OK. Mark is going to look after
them so you and I can have a bit of time
together. I'll go and get my design book."

I watched as Mum shut the door behind
her. I was glad we were talking again and it
would be fun designing the cake, but I didn't

feel like everything was completely back to normal.

I swallowed. Oh, if only things could be how they used to be.

Really? Did I really want that? If I could wave a magic wand, would I go back to my old life – just Mum and me and no bakery?

No. I knew I wouldn't.

Mum came back in and I made myself smile at her. There was a *new* normal now – I just had to get used to it.

9

When I woke next morning, I was filled
with a new determination. I was going to be
grown-up and helpful. No more feeling sorry
for myself. It was Day Three at the Sugar and
Spice Bakery and I was going to do all I could
to help Mum make it a success.

When I arrived at the bakery I was pleased
to see we had three customers already. Three
people was a lot better than an empty shop!

I took off my coat and caught sight of a
clipboard with a sheet of paper on the counter.
It showed a picture of lots of women in belly-
dancing costumes. The heading read, "SIX-
HOUR SPONSORED BELLY DANCE!"

"It's the sponsorship forms for my belly

dance," said Paula, as the final customer left. "We're doing it this Sunday."

I added my name to the form. "You've got loads of people already," I said, noticing that several sheets had already been filled in.

"It's for a good cause," said Paula. "Lots of people know about Tom."

She took her purse out of her bag behind the counter and showed me a photo.

Tom had dark hair and brown eyes like Paula. He was smiling broadly at the camera, but I could see he was very thin. "He's so brave," Paula said, sadness catching in her voice. "Always smiling. The whole family was devastated when he was diagnosed." She sighed and put the photo back in her bag. "The doctors say that if he has this operation, he has a chance of a normal life. Maybe you'd like to come along and belly dance too?" She swung her hips at me.

I grinned. "I think I'll stick to sponsoring you." I wanted to do something to help, but I wasn't quite ready to bare my belly to all of Ashingham.

Just then the doorbell tinkled. I looked around and saw Mia coming in.

"Hi!" I cried.

She looked very surprised. I could have kicked myself. I'd been hoping she would come in again so I could find out more about her, but of course there was no reason she would have given me, a random girl she met in a bakery, a second's thought.

"Hi," she said, then looked away.

Feeling embarrassed, I went back to rearranging the bread baskets. Maybe the others were right and she *was* unfriendly. To my astonishment, Mia followed me. She hovered for a moment and then took a deep breath. "Um . . . what are the different types of bread?" she asked, the words coming out in a rush.

I blinked. It was an odd question for someone who obviously knew something about baking. But as I looked at Mia standing there, half-awkwardly, half-hopefully, it dawned on me that maybe she'd just wanted an excuse to start a conversation.

"Well, those are the farmhouse white and granary loaves," I said. "And then the others are the speciality breads."

"Like what?" she asked.

I pointed to each bread in turn. "Sourdough, ciabatta, brioche and raisin and walnut bread," I recited.

Sourdough - great with soup or cheese or just to eat warm, with butter. (My fave!)

Ciabatta - really nice with cold meats, makes a great sandwich or cut into wedges and eaten with dips.

Brioche - a sweet bread, like a cross between bread and cake, lovely for breakfast or when toasted with paté.

Raisin and walnut bread - sweet and heavy, just needs butter, can be toasted too or served with cheese.

I tried to think of something else to say. "Have you ever made bread?"

Mia nodded. "Yes. I love making it. You're so lucky to have a mum who's a baker." The words came out quickly. "My mum only ever cooks ready meals and buys cakes and biscuits in shops. Well, unless I make them. My gran taught me how to bake."

I felt a rush of excitement. Maybe Mia did have friend potential after all. "What's your favourite thing to bake?" I asked her.

"Cupcakes and cookies."

"Me too!" I said. "And millionaire's shortbread."

"Yes, and gingerbread," added Mia, grinning, her awkwardness melting away like butter in a hot frying pan.

"Mince pies," I said. "And jam tarts."

"Actually, everything!" She grinned.

"Do . . . do you want to stay and help here for a while?" I said impulsively.

Mia's eyes widened. "Yes, please! I'd love to! I'll just ring my mum so she doesn't wonder where I am. She owns the wedding dress shop down the road. I said I'd come and get some pastries for us. I have to help her in the shop most days in the holidays." She looked around wistfully. "I'd much rather help out at a bakery."

Mia made a quick call to her mum, who said it was fine if she stayed. "So, what do we have to do?" Mia asked.

"It's easy. We just help Paula wrap things up and keep the shelves and baskets looking tidy and answer any questions people have."

"What if I get things wrong?" said Mia.

"You won't," I reassured her. "You'll be fine."

At first we just tidied the shelves but then the bakery got a little busier and we went to stand behind the counter. Mia went bright red whenever people asked her anything. She was really shy, so most of the time I did the talking while she wrapped things up.

After a while, we had a break for lunch. We sat on the stools by the window and I had a doughnut and Mia had a slice of lemon cake. All her signs of stand-offishness seemed to have disappeared. We chatted as if we'd known each other for ages.

I wondered what sort of pastry or cake or bread Mia would be, but I just couldn't decide. Definitely not something flaky like a croissant or show-offy like a chocolate éclair. Maybe a lemon tart? No, lemon was too sharp. That wasn't right. Nothing seemed to quite fit. I obviously needed to get to know her better before I decided.

We talked about school. Mia told me she hated it. "I loved primary school," she sighed. "But King William's is horrible."

"Why?"

She shrugged. "People just ignore me or pick on me. I never really know what to talk about to them, so I don't say anything and then they call me stuck-up. Tegan McGarrity's the worst. She's in Year Seven."

"I met her yesterday," I said.

Mia shuddered. "I try to stay out of her way but she always seems to find me."

I frowned. "What about your friends? Don't they stand up for you?"

"I . . . I don't really have any friends." Mia played with the crumbs from her cake. "I wish you were in my form."

"We can still be friends even if we're not in the same form," I told her.

Her eyes lit up. "Can we?"

"Of course," I said. "We can hang out at lunchtime and stuff." I had a sudden idea. "Why don't you come to my house tomorrow morning? Mark – my stepdad – is working from home in the morning so we could do some baking together and then, if you want, you could come and help me on Saturday?" I told her about the farmers' market and my plans to give out leaflets and samples of cakes.

She blinked. "You mean, just go up to people in the street?"

"Yes."

"I don't know. I hate talking to strangers," she said.

I thought for a moment. "Well, how about you come along and just hand out the leaflets? I'll do the talking. Please come. Mark will be there, but it'll be much more fun if you come too."

She looked pleased. "OK. I'd like to help."

I felt like hugging her. Despite what I'd said to Mum about not minding going to the market on my own, it would be so much better to have a friend with me as well as Mark. "Thank you!"

As we said goodbye, I bubbled with happiness. Mia might be a bit shy, but once you got her talking she was really nice. She wasn't unfriendly at all. And she loved baking. I couldn't wait to get to know her better.

What could we bake tomorrow? Brownies, maybe? Jam tarts? Biscuits? Cupcakes?

So, Day Three was a success. I've got a morning of baking with a new friend to look forward to, and someone to help me on Saturday. Things are definitely looking up!

10

"Hi." Mia stood on the doorstep next morning. She avoided my eyes and looked at the ground.

"Hi!" I'd been looking forward to seeing Mia since we said goodbye yesterday. It was going to be awesome. I'd decided we'd bake cupcakes and cookies, because Mia had said those were her favourites – and they were easy. "Come on in. I've got all the ingredients ready."

"OK." Mia came inside and slipped off her coat.

"Just chuck it on the stairs," I told her.

She put the coat down awkwardly. Her

shyness from the day before seemed to have come back.

"I thought we could make cookies and cakes," I said.

She nodded.

"I love making cupcakes, don't you?" I said. I felt like I was talking too much to fill the quiet. "Decorating them is definitely the best bit, isn't it?"

Mia didn't say anything. My heart sank. What if yesterday had been a one-off? What if she didn't talk ALL morning?

"The kitchen's this way," I said.

The kitchen is one of my favourite rooms in the house. It's L-shaped, with cream cupboards and a brand new cooker. At the far end, it turns a corner and that's where we have a seating area with a large pine table and French windows that open out to the garden. Mark was upstairs in the study. He'd said to shout if we needed him, but otherwise he'd keep out of the way.

"I thought we could do the cupcakes first."
I went over to the table and pushed the flour,
butter and sugar towards her. "Why don't
you measure these out?"

Mia washed her hands and then started to
weigh out the flour and sugar. "So . . . um
. . . what type of cupcakes are we making?"
she asked.

"How about we do some plain vanilla but
also make some rose and apple-blossom cakes
too," I suggested. I'd thought, since we were

doing easy recipes, we could try different flavours that Mia might not have tasted before. "Does that sound OK?"

Mia looked interested. "I've never made rose or apple-blossom cupcakes. They sound cool."

I seized on the fact that we had finally found something to talk about. "They are. They're amazing! And when we've baked them we can decorate them too. Mum's got loads of decorating stuff. Look!" I pulled open a massive pine cupboard behind the table, revealing a huge selection of icing sugar, food colouring, sprinkle toppings, edible glitter and ready-made decorations, as well as piping bags, palette knives and every type of piping nozzle.

"Wow!" Mia's eyes looked as if they were going to pop out of her head. "Can we use any of these things?"

"Yeah." I glanced at her and risked teasing. "But, you know, we have to actually MAKE the cakes first."

She caught my eye and grinned, looking a lot more like the Mia from the day before. "Sorry. It's just awesome. It's like being in a decorating shop!"

I picked up a spatula and brandished it at her. "Decorating later, Mia. Now . . ." I channelled the presenters from my favourite TV show, *Junior British Baker*, "Let's bake!"

She giggled and I felt the tension between us ease. We set to work.

"Time for the whisking," I said, handing Mia an electric whisk. "Do you want to do this bit?"

"OK," she said.

She took the whisk and hit the button, but she must have hit the highest setting by mistake. Mixture splattered everywhere and she shrieked before turning the whisk off.

Cake batter dripped down the walls and we both had splodges on our faces. There was silence. Then I giggled as I saw Mia's horrified expression. "You should see your face!"

Mia started to giggle too. "You should see *yours*!"

We both burst out laughing.

"I'm really sorry!" said Mia. "I'll clear it up."

"That's all right. We can both do it. Then you can carry on whisking. But you see this little button here, Mia?" I said. "You just push it a little way to the first notch so it turns the whisk on but makes it go *slowly*. OK?"

She flicked a bit of mixture at me. "All right, Miss Know-It-All," she said. "Why don't you get on with making the biscuits?"

I saluted. "On to it, captain!"

MY BEST CUPCAKE RECIPE

Ingredients

125g unsalted butter

175g caster sugar

225g plain flour

3 large eggs

½ teaspoon baking powder

¼ teaspoon salt
80ml cream
2 teaspoons vanilla extract or
other flavouring

Equipment you will need

Muffin tray
12 cupcake cases

What to do

1. Preheat oven to 170°C.

2. In a bowl, stir the flour, baking powder and salt together. Put to one side.

3. In a large bowl, cream the butter and sugar until pale. Add one egg at a time, mixing well and scraping down the sides of the bowl before adding another egg.

4. Add the flour mixture along with the cream and vanilla extract (or other flavouring).

Mix with a hand-held mixer or spatula until everything is all mixed in together, but don't keep on mixing too long or the cakes will be chewy.

5. Put the cases in the muffin tray and fill the cases three-quarters full.

6. Put in the oven and bake for about 30 minutes or until they are light golden on top.

7. Take them out of the oven, put them on a wire rack to cool and wait until they have completely cooled before decorating.

From that moment on, everything was fine. Mia and I worked happily side by side. Sometimes we chatted, sometimes we giggled and made jokes, and at other times we just mixed ingredients in companionable silence.

In the warmth of the kitchen, with the smell of cupcakes baking filling the air, it was strange to remember that I had worried how our morning would turn out.

Later, while our cookies and cupcakes cooled, we got out the decorating ingredients. We decided to keep the cookies simple and coat them with white icing and a light dusting of edible glitter.

"What about the cupcakes?" I asked, looking at them. They were what Mum called "a good bake" – they had rounded, even tops with no jagged peaks or, even worse, sunken centres. They looked yummy. "Buttercream frosting or icing made from icing sugar and water?"

Mia considered it. "Well, buttercream frosting always looks really pretty but actually I prefer to eat cakes with icing just made with icing sugar and water."

I agreed. "Me too – let's do that. We could put thick icing on and top them with sugar flowers."

We decided to make white flowers with green leaves for the apple-blossom cake and

pink rosebuds for the rose-flavoured cakes,
but it wasn't easy.

"What do you think?" I asked her, holding
up my attempt. "It's not great, is it?"

"It looks like
a squashed
strawberry!"
Mia said. "But
it's better than
mine. Look!"
She pointed at the
flower head on her chopping board – it had
drooping, uneven petals and a bright yellow
centre. "It's an alien!"

"Maybe we should use some of Mum's
ready-made ones," I said. "I'll ask her to give
us a lesson on how to make them one day."
Although secretly I wondered when she'd
ever find the time.

"Yes please!" said Mia.

We used a spoon to cover the cakes. We
carefully placed the little flowers on the top.

We stepped back admiringly. "They look
really good," said Mia.

"But do they taste good?" I said.

Mia grinned. "Only one way to find out!"

After we had cleared up, we took some cakes and biscuits upstairs for Mark and he declared them delicious. There were lots left over so I suggested we took some around to Mrs Rees. Secretly I hoped Alice would be there and she could get a chance to see that Mia wasn't stuck-up after all.

"Hello, Hannah. What a nice surprise," Mrs Rees said, opening the door. "And who's this?"

"This is Mia," I said loudly. "She goes to King William's too." I turned to Mia. "Mrs Rees is Alice's grandma – Alice Young, in my class."

"Oh," said Mia, making the connection.

"We've been baking, Mrs Rees," I went on. "We thought you might like to try some of our cookies and cupcakes. We've made far too many for us to eat."

Mrs Rees beamed. "They look really delicious. Thank you so much. I should be giving you some money."

"Oh no. They're a gift," I said, handing them to her. "Is Alice here?"

Mrs Rees shook her head. "I'm afraid not. I'll tell her you called round though. And when you next go to the bakery, will you tell Paula I'm coming to the town hall on Sunday to watch that sponsored belly dance of hers?" She shook her head. "Her poor nephew. I hope they raise a lot of money."

"Me too," I said. "Bye, Mrs Rees."

"What's the matter with Paula's nephew?" Mia asked as we walked back to my house.

I explained.

"That's awful," Mia said.

"I know. She's doing this sponsored belly dance on Sunday to raise money. I wish I could do something to help."

"Well . . ." Mia paused. "How about we sell cakes at the belly dance? We've got loads left from today and it hasn't taken us long at all. I bet the people watching would love to buy cakes, especially if they knew it was for charity."

I stared at her. "That's brilliant!" It really was. I could hardly believe that quiet, shy Mia had come up with such a great idea. The more time I spent with her, the more I liked her. "We should ask Paula!"

"What about buying the ingredients, though?" Mia said. "That might be expensive."

"I'll ask Mum. She gets everything cheaper because of the shop. I bet she'll give us what we need. It's for such a good cause."

Mia's eyes shone. "Let's go and ask your mum and Paula right now!"

11

Mia and I decided to take a few of our leftover cakes and biscuits to the bakery for Mum and Paula to try. It was quiet in the shop again, and Mum and Paula listened to our idea.

"It's so kind of you to offer," Paula said. She munched a biscuit. "And these are really delicious! I'd love you to have a cake stall."

"I'll bring the ingredients home for you," said Mum. "Just let me know what you need. I could come and help too, actually. The bakery will be closed on Sunday."

Mia and I jumped up and down with excitement. It was really going to happen!

"I knew something good was coming my

way today," Paula said. "My horoscope said that Sagittarians should expect kind deeds." She waved her finger at us. "You see, girls, the stars are always right! The idea must have come from them."

Mia nudged me as Paula went back behind the counter. "So that's why I thought of it," she whispered. "The stars were talking to me and I didn't realise!"

I bit back a giggle.

There was a tinkle of a bell as the door opened. I looked around. "Alice!" I said. She was with two other girls, one dark-haired and one blonde.

"Hey, Hannah! I thought I'd bring Misha and Lara to meet you."

"Hi, I'm Hannah." I smiled at the other girls.

MISHA: dark hair and brown eyes. She has three sisters, she's outgoing, into singing, dancing and ponies. What pastry would she be? A centre-of-attention, fun strawberry-cream tart.

LARA: blonde hair, green eyes and freckles. An only child, quieter than Misha, a bit more sensible, into art and ponies. What pastry would she be? A blueberry muffin – not as showy as Misha, but really nice.

"You know Mia, don't you?" I said, pulling Mia forward.

"Yeah," Misha said. "We're in the same maths set."

Alice smiled. "Hi, Mia."

"Hi," Mia said, stepping back and crossing her arms over her chest. I was beginning to see why the others thought she was stuck-up. Her body language was screaming out that she wanted to be left alone.

Alice turned to me. "We're all going to Harry's – the ice-cream parlour on the high street. Do you want to come?"

"Yeah, we heard what happened at the park," said Lara. "Classic!"

"I wish I'd been there," Misha agreed. "Go on, come for an ice cream. Your mum won't mind, will she?"

I was uncomfortably aware they were just talking to me and not Mia. I really wanted them to include her too. "OK," I said. "I'd love to. Do you want to come too, Mia?"

Mia shook her head. "I can't. I have to go back and help my mum at the shop."

"Oh, go on, come with us!" I said. I knew she didn't really have to go back. She'd been with me all morning. I looked at Alice.

"Yeah, come on," she said, taking the hint. "It'll be fun, Mia."

Mia shook her head again. "No, thanks. Bye," she said abruptly, then slipped out through the door before I could stop her.

I didn't understand it. She sounded so rude. No wonder the others weren't keen to be friends with her. OK, I knew it was just because she felt awkward, but they didn't.

Misha grinned at me. "You're going to love Harry's! It's awesome."

"Their ice-cream sodas are the best," said Lara.

"What are we waiting for?" said Alice.

"Wait a sec." I ran through to the kitchen. Mum said it was fine and gave me some money and then I hurried to join the others.

To get to Harry's, we had to walk by Mia's mum's shop on the high street. I glanced in the window as we passed and saw Mia sitting by the counter as her mum served a customer.

She was resting her chin on her hands. Our eyes met. "Come with us!" I mouthed. But she shook her head. I gave up. I couldn't physically drag her for an ice cream.

"So how come you know Mia?" Misha said as we walked on.

"She came into the bakery and we got talking," I said. "She came to my house this morning and we did some baking together."

The others exchanged looks. "You're honoured, then," said Misha sarcastically. "She always just ignores us."

"It's because she's shy," I said.

"Stuck-up, you mean. She thinks she's too good for us," Misha replied.

"No." I could feel my heart beating a bit faster. I didn't want to fall out with them when they had made an effort to be friendly, but I didn't want them to be mean about Mia either. "She's nice when you get to know her. She *is* just shy."

I held Misha's gaze. I knew I mustn't back down or she'd think I was a pushover who just agreed with everything other people said.

After a moment, she shrugged. "OK, if you say so."

"I don't know her at all," Lara said. "She never says anything at school."

Alice seemed to sense I was feeling awkward and changed the subject. "So, what's your favourite flavour of ice cream? Mine's butterscotch."

I was grateful. It felt good to be out with them. I just wished Mia could be with us too.

The ice-cream parlour *was* amazing. Harry's has every flavour you can think of, and it's decorated like an old-fashioned American diner, with vintage signs and booths for seating. It's got a music player in one corner and two massive counters full of ice creams and sorbets. I decided to have a mango ice-cream soda, which is mango ice cream mixed with lemonade and pieces of fresh mango. The top of it all foamed up with creamy half-melted ice cream. It was delicious.

As we sat down in one of the booths, Misha and Lara asked me

stuff about my old school and the bakery.
Then Alice started talking about horses and
the riding school they went to and about some
of the people they knew there. They told
funny stories and teased each other. They're
quite different personalities – Misha is pretty
loud, Lara more quiet and smiley, and Alice is
somewhere in the middle – but together they
make a really good group. They remind me of
how Issy, Lucy and I are when we're together.
It's like mixing up lots of different ingredients
to make a really good cake.

When they found out I knew nothing about
ponies, Misha kept teasing me and asking
questions like, "What's a chestnut?" When I
said it's a nut you can roast and which tastes
amazing in chocolate cake or mousse, they
thought it was the funniest thing ever, because
apparently a chestnut is the colour of a horse
and also a bit of hard skin on the inside of
a horse's leg. I didn't mind them laughing,
though – they weren't doing it in a mean way
and it made me feel like part of the group.
I got my own back as well by testing their

baking knowledge. They all thought a truffle was a type of chocolate and had no idea it was also a type of mushroom that could be used in bread or pastries or expensive oils. Alice said she'd always wondered why people on TV cookery shows grated truffles into main course dishes like pasta and soup.

Suddenly a new track came on the jukebox. "I love this song!" said Misha. She grabbed the spoon from her banana split and started using it as a microphone, singing along.

"Sorry," Alice groaned. "She always does this." She and Lara threw balled-up paper napkins at Misha until she stopped. Then we saw the waitress looking at us disapprovingly and decided to clear up. I was having so much fun: I couldn't believe it when I looked at my phone and saw we'd been there an hour.

"I'd better get back and help Mum," I said. And I couldn't help feeling a bit guilty about leaving Mia. I thought I should maybe call into her mum's shop later and see if she was OK.

Misha smiled. "I'm glad you're coming to King William's."

Alice and Lara nodded.

"Let's try and meet up again this week," said Alice. "We're having a sleepover at mine tomorrow. Why don't you come, Hannah?"

"I'd love to," I said. "But I can't." I explained about the farmers' market. "I have to get everything ready."

"It sounds fun," said Lara.

Misha and Alice nodded.

"You could come along and help me," I said. "There's free cake in it!"

"I'm supposed to be seeing my gran. But I'm sure she wouldn't mind," said Alice. "I'll let you know."

"I think I'm free," said Misha, and Lara nodded too.

"Brilliant." I got to my feet and left some money on the table, feeling light and happy. "See you then, maybe."

"Bye!" they chorused.

I knew that as soon as I'd gone, they'd probably start talking about me, because that's what I'd have done with Lucy and Issy, but the good thing was that they seemed to like me. And I liked them. A thought struck me. What was Mia going to say when I told her I'd invited them along on Saturday? I had a feeling she wasn't going to like it.

My tummy gave a nervous lurch. What if Mia decided not to come if they were there? Or what if she did come, but was really rude again and Alice, Misha and Lara decided they definitely didn't like her? I'd promised Mia I would hang out with her at school – and I really wanted to – but I also wanted to be friends with Alice, Misha and Lara. I began to wish I hadn't invited them after all, but it was too late to go back and change things now. All I could do was wait and see what happened.

12

As I passed Mia's mum's shop on the way back, I peered in, but I couldn't see Mia. To my surprise, when I pushed open the bakery door, I saw her behind the counter with Paula. There seemed to be a mini rush on for once, and a queue of about eight people. My heart leaped. I'd never seen so many people in the shop! "Hi," I said to Mia and Paula. There wasn't time to say any more. I washed my hands and started to help too.

As I helped serve the customers, I realised I was starting to recognise some of them. Neil, the birdwatcher, was now coming in every day to buy a sausage roll or a couple of cheesy twists. Dennis, who was always very gloomy, often came in too, to buy a fresh loaf and something sweet for his tea – either a fruit tart or a meringue. Then there was Harmony, who wore long skirts and lots of scarves and liked to discuss horoscopes with Paula. She bought something different for her tea every day. And then there was another lady who knew Paula, who called in to the bakery on the way to taking her son, George, to his tennis lessons. He seemed to have them every day. I wondered if he ever had time to see his friends!

I handed Neil his cheesy twist in a bag. "What bird are you looking for today?" I asked him.

"Someone thinks they've spotted a yellow-headed yellow wagtail," he said. He shook his head. "It's probably a British yellow wagtail, though, don't you think?"

"Um . . . yeah," I said. "Well, good luck!"

I smiled as he left. I liked him despite his weirdness. In fact, I really liked talking to all the customers. The bakery had been open less than a week but already I was beginning to feel part of Ashingham life. I hoped the advertising worked and that the bakery became so busy that Mum could stop worrying all the time.

When the queue died down, Mia and I began tidying the counter. She didn't mention me going for an ice cream. It was like there was a big obstacle between us. Finally, I couldn't stay silent any longer.

"You should have come for an ice cream. It was fun."

Mia didn't reply.

"You should," I insisted. "Alice, Misha and Lara are really nice. If you got to know them, you'd have more friends at school."

Mia shrugged. "I don't need more friends."

I raised my eyebrows. I didn't believe her. She saw my look.

"I don't! I'm happy the way I am!" She moved to the bread baskets and started to tidy them.

I glanced at Paula. She nodded at Mia's back, gesturing for me to go after her. "She's a Pisces," she whispered. "They can be very touchy. Go on!"

I went after Mia. "I just think you should try and get to know them."

"Why? I've told you, I'm fine," she said.

I didn't want to fall out with her. "OK, look, I'm sorry."

She hesitated and then sighed. "I'm sorry too. I didn't mean to snap. I just don't find it that easy to make friends. I'm no good at talking to people I don't know. I never know what to say." She turned and gave me a small smile. "I don't even know why YOU want to be friends with me."

"It's a complete mystery," I said, rolling my eyes. "Maybe it's because I LIKE you."

Her smile broadened. "Yeah, you like me because I do all the work around here." She gestured to the baskets. "These aren't going to tidy themselves, you know."

"All right, all right," I said.

As we tidied I thought about telling her I'd invited the others to help on Saturday. But after her outburst I was worried she would freak out. I'd tell her later, I decided.

In between helping Paula whenever a customer came in, Mia and I sat down and made a list of everything we would make for the Sunday cake stall and the ingredients we would need.

We decided to do cupcakes again – some with thick royal icing and others with piped buttercream. Mum offered to make some more flower decorations and promised to give us both a lesson in how to make them when she had a bit of time on her hands. I couldn't help wondering when that would be.

THINGS TO MAKE FOR THE CAKE STALL

 Vanilla cupcakes

Apple-blossom cupcakes

Rose cupcakes

Lemon cupcakes

Chocolate cupcakes

Plain shortbread biscuits

Mia and I stayed at the bakery until closing time and then Mia went back to her mum's shop. I still hadn't plucked up the courage to admit that I had asked Alice, Misha and Lara to come on Saturday. Every time I thought about mentioning it, my mouth went dry and I found I couldn't speak.

Maybe it will all work out really well, I thought. Mia will get over her shyness and talk to them and they'll see how nice she is. But then maybe Mia will stomp off in a huff like she did today and Misha will call her stuck-up again . . .

I cringed. What was going to happen?

As Mum and I walked home together that evening with the leftover pastries in bags we talked about the bakery. She was pleased because the lady who wanted the dinosaur birthday cake had come in and loved all the designs we'd done and asked Mum to make the cake that was a model of a brontosaurus for her son. She'd also brought a friend in who wanted a wedding cake with a rose and lily theme.

"I think this might be the start of a turnaround, you know," said Mum.

"I'm sure it is," I said, linking my hand through her arm. "And I'm sure the farmers' market is going to help too."

"I hope so," said Mum. "We can't go on as we are doing."

We passed a shop with a display of bags in the window and it made me remember something. "Ooh, I need a new bag for school, remember? Can we get one before Monday?"

Mum nodded. "You're right, we do need to do some shopping. You need some tights as well – and some black PE shorts." She glanced at me. "How are you feeling about school now? You seem to be making a few new friends."

"I am . . . I think."

"You think?"

I hesitated. I really wanted to tell her that the friends I was making didn't seem to want to be friends with each other and I was worried I was going to end up caught in the middle and upsetting everyone, but should I say anything? Mum had enough problems of her own right now – she didn't need to be worrying about my problems too. But I really wanted to tell her.

"Everything is OK, isn't it?" Mum said.

I shrugged. "Yeah."

"Well, that's good," Mum said, sounding relieved.

I had the sudden horrible feeling that I was one more thing on a list in her head that she had to do: *Check Hannah's OK. Tick.*

"Now, how about this wedding cake design?" Mum went on. "I thought maybe I could make sugar lilies and roses and have them tumbling down the cake. What do you think?"

"That sounds nice," I said quietly.

"And the edging around the base of each tier could be tiny leaves, maybe dusted with edible glitter?"

"Yeah."

Listening to Mum talking about her cake ideas, I was glad I hadn't said anything. It's so rare for Mum and me to be on our own at the moment, I didn't want to spoil it by telling her about my worries.

"How about different flavoured sponges for the different tiers?" I suggested. "A plain sponge, maybe a chocolate sponge and something delicate like a rose-flavoured sponge?"

"Oh yes, I like that idea," said Mum. "I'll need to find out the bride and groom's favourite flavours."

"And maybe add ribbons in colours to

match the bridesmaids' dresses?"

We talked about the cake all the way home.
It was fun, like how we used to be. But at the
same time, not telling her about Mia and the
others made me feel just that little bit further
away from her. As if we were on two separate
boats on the ocean, drifting apart.

13

That night I phoned Alice to find out what sort of bag and shoes everyone had at King William's in case it was different from my old school. She was really helpful, warning me that no one wore shoes with any type of strap across the foot at King William's, and telling me my bag needed to have something bright on it and not to do up my tie too tightly. I was very glad to have her advice. There are just so many mistakes to make when you start a new school. She even offered to come and help me choose a school bag the next morning. I was really pleased, and we arranged to meet at eleven.

Luckily Mia had a dentist appointment so

there was no danger of Alice seeing her and mentioning the farmers' market. Alice and I walked to the shops on the high street, where she helped me choose a bag. Mum had said she'd nip out later and get my tights and PE shorts. It was fun shopping together. We went to the make-up section of the pharmacy and tried on different lip glosses and perfume, just like Lucy, Issy and I had done last time we'd been shopping, just before I'd moved.

After lunch at the bakery, I went back home. Mark was there working and Mia was going to come round so we could bake for the cake sale on Sunday.

As soon as Mia walked through the door I knew something was wrong. She was pale and looked as if she'd been crying.

"What's the matter?" I said. "Are you OK?"

She dumped her bag on the floor. "I bumped into Tegan McGarrity and her friends on the way here." She rubbed her eyes.

"What happened?"

Mia shrugged. "The usual. Tegan grabbed my bag and threw it around to her friends and wouldn't let me have it back until everything fell out. Then Tegan took the money from my purse."

"What? Didn't someone see?" I couldn't believe it.

"There wasn't anyone around," said Mia. "I only had £1.20, though."

"It's still stealing," I said. "You've got to tell someone."

Mia looked alarmed. "No way. Can you imagine how much she'd go after me if I did? Forget it," she sighed. "She makes threats and stuff, but she's never actually hurt me and it wasn't much money."

"She needs to be stopped. It's not fair." I gave Mia a hug. "Come on, let's start baking and you can forget all about it."

Mia managed a smile. "Baking's good for that."

We went into the kitchen and started weighing and measuring, mixing and stirring. As we worked and chatted, Mia seemed to cheer up. Once the cakes were in the oven and the kitchen was filling with the delicious scent of baking, we made shortbread biscuits.

MY RECIPE FOR SHORTBREAD BISCUITS

Ingredients

40g caster sugar

15g powdered icing sugar

115g salted butter diced and at room temperature

130g plain flour and extra flour for rolling out

40g ground rice or fine semolina (if you don't have either of these use an extra 35g of plain flour instead)

What to do

1. Preheat the oven to 150°C.

2. Put the butter in a bowl and beat it with a wooden spoon until it is soft.

Beat in the sugar pressing it against the side of the bowl.

3. Sift the flour and ground rice into the butter and sugar and mix to a smooth dough, then bring it together into a ball with your hands. Wrap the ball of dough in cling film and put in the fridge for at least 15 minutes.

4. Line a baking tray with baking parchment, then take the dough out of the fridge. Lightly roll it out on a floured surface. Cut shapes (about 3mm thick) with round biscuit cutters and then place them on the baking tray.

5. Cook them in the middle of the oven at 150°C for about 30 minutes or until they are a light golden colour.

6. Take out and leave to cool, then eat!!

MY TOP TIPS FOR MAKING
SHORTBREAD BISCUITS

1. Don't mix the dough too much or the biscuits will end up tough and hard.
2. The dough needs to be cold when you roll it out. If it gets warm, wrap it in cling film and put it back in the fridge for 10 minutes.

"Are the leaflets all ready for tomorrow?" Mia asked.

I nodded. "Mark had them done at the printer's. They look brilliant." They did – all glossy and professional. "He's going to drop the twins off and meet us at the market at ten o'clock. Apparently if we want to give out samples we need to get there by ten at the latest to get a spot. They only have limited space for people who aren't regulars." I felt guilt twist inside me as I thought about my secret. *Tell her about Alice, Lara and Misha.*

Tell her now. But I couldn't. Maybe I could get away with pretending they'd turned up out of the blue?

"And you'll do most of the talking to people," Mia said. "I'll just hand out the samples and leaflets."

"You could talk to people too, you know," I said. "You like chatting to the customers in the bakery now."

"Talking to strangers in the street is completely different to talking to people in the bakery," Mia said.

"How is it?" I looked at her in frustration. "I don't get it. How is it that you're fine with me and Paula and Mum, and the customers in the bakery, but you can't talk to people on the street?"

"I don't know!" Mia's voice rose. "You're not shy, Hannah. You don't know what it's like. If you say I have to talk to strangers on the street tomorrow, I'm not coming!" There was silence for a moment. "Promise you won't make me?"

"All right. I promise," I said. "But you

140

could at least try talking to Alice, Misha and Lara when you next see them," I said.

Mia didn't reply.

I gave up. "Come on, we should get the shortbread out."

As we laid the biscuits on wire trays to cool, I sneaked a glance at Mia. Maybe I was wrong to try and change her. After all, friends should accept each other the way they are, shouldn't they?

But I remembered the wistful way she'd looked at me the other day when I walked past her mum's shop with Alice, Misha and Lara. She did want to make friends, I was sure of it. The trouble was she just didn't know how.

That night, Mum stayed on at the shop to meet the bride to discuss the rose and lily wedding cake. Mark was trying to finish off some work so I offered to get the twins their tea. We made mini toad-in-the-holes together.

Molly and Ella had just finished wolfing them down when we heard Mum's key in the lock. The twins ran to meet her.

"We've been cooking with Hannah!" said Molly.

"We cooked toad with mould," Ella told her.

Mum raised her eyebrows.

"Toad-in-the-hole," I corrected.

Mum smiled. "Ah, I should have guessed. Thanks, sweetheart. That was lovely of you. Where's Mark?"

"Upstairs working," I said. "How was the bakery?"

"About the same," said Mum, stretching. "Ouch!" she said, massaging a shoulder. "Goodness, I hadn't realised how much carrying there would be. Shifting the sacks of flour and those big metal trays really takes it out of me. There always seems to be so much to do."

"What about my school stuff?" I asked anxiously. "My tights and shorts? Did you get those?"

Mum clapped a hand to her forehead. "Oh no! I forgot!"

"Mum! I need them for Monday. I can't go to school without them."

"I'm sorry, sweetheart," said Mum. She put an arm around my shoulders. "Look, don't worry. I'll nip out tomorrow."

Tears stung my eyes. I couldn't believe she'd forgotten. I swallowed hard. *Be grown-up, be grown-up.* "It's OK," I said. "I'll go in the morning with Mia before the farmers' market."

"No, no, no. You shouldn't have to go out and get your own school uniform. I'll do it, Hannah," she said. "I'll go in the afternoon once the baking's all done – oh no! I've got a meeting with my supplier—"

I cut her short. "I'm ten, Mum, not two. I can go." I didn't want to risk her forgetting again or running out of time.

Mum hesitated and then gave a reluctant nod. "All right. It probably makes sense. You and Mia can go together. I'll give you the money in the morning."

I nodded and went to the stairs.

"Where are you going?" Mum asked in surprise.

"To have a shower." I really didn't feel like talking to her any more.

I went to the bathroom and turned the shower on. Stepping in, I let my mind go blank, concentrating on the feel of the water beating down on my head. When I got out, I wrapped a towel around myself and headed for my bedroom.

Mum came up the stairs. "Hannah, sweetie, when you're changed do you want to have a chat about that wedding cake? The bride made some good suggestions today when she came in."

I knew she felt guilty but, for once, I didn't feel like talking to Mum about cake designs. I didn't want to be grown-up and responsible. I just wanted to curl up in my room. I shook my head. "I'm tired," I said. "I think I'm going to read for a bit."

"Oh. Are you sure? Do you want anything? A hot chocolate? A snack?" said

Mum. She looked disappointed.

"No, thanks."

I saw her frown and take a step towards me, reaching out. "Hannah?"

"Night, Mum," I said. I went into my room and shut the door.

I heard her hesitate on the landing, and then the sound of her footsteps going slowly downstairs.

14

From the moment I woke up on Saturday I felt like the White Rabbit from *Alice in Wonderland* – the one who's always running around saying "I'm late, I'm late!" Nothing seemed to run smoothly. At breakfast, the twins had a fight about who would have the last of the peanut butter on their toast. Then, as Mark was packing the car, he dropped one of the boxes, and leaflets spilled everywhere. We had to hurry around grabbing them all. By the time Mark was ready to set off with the twins, I hadn't even had time to get dressed, so I told him I'd walk to the bakery and meet him there.

When I went upstairs, I found my favourite

jeans and blue cupcake
t-shirt at the bottom of
the laundry basket, which
was overflowing with dirty
washing. Argh! I'd *told* Mum
I needed those for today.
Feeling cross, I pulled on
a different pair of jeans
(which I didn't like half as
much) and a white t-shirt
with stars on, then set off.

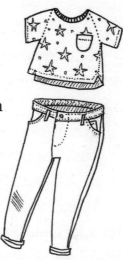

I ran down the road.
Everything I had to do was jumping around
in my head and I was ten minutes late for
meeting Mia already. Not a good start to the
day at all!

"Listen, Hannah, I've been thinking about it.
I'll buy your shorts and tights," Mum said.
"You shouldn't have to do it."

I shook my head. Mia and I still just about
had time to get my school things before

meeting Mark. "It's OK, Mum, honestly," I told her. "We'll run."

We hurried out of the bakery. "So where do we need to go to get your school things?" Mia said

"Mum said to try the department store."

What Mum hadn't said was how big the store was and how hard it was to find the right section. When we eventually did find the sports section, there were no PE shorts left in my size, so we had to try three other shops before we managed to buy some. I could feel my heart beating faster with every shop we went into. As we left the final shop with the shorts, I looked at my watch. We only had ten minutes to drop this stuff back at the bakery and get to the market.

"Quick! Let's go!" I said, darting around some pedestrians. We dodged past more people, buggies and dogs along the high street and finally ran down the quiet street to the bakery. It was only then I spotted that my left shoelace had come undone. Annoying, but there was no time to stop and tie it.

Big mistake. My right foot landed on my left shoelace, and suddenly I fell forward, arms flailing. BANG! My hands met the hard concrete as I crashed to the ground.

"Hannah!" I heard Mia shriek.

I lay on the pavement for a moment, too shocked to move. I was aware my hands were hurting, and my knees and . . . OUCH! I tried to get up and pain shot through my left ankle.

"Hannah? Hannah?" Mia crouched beside me. "Are you OK?"

Was I OK? I felt a bit dizzy. I wasn't sure whether it was from the fall or from the pain in my ankle.

"Ouch." I looked at my palms. They were scraped and bleeding, pieces of grit embedded in the skin. The right knee of my jeans was ripped and through the rip I could see another scrape. But it was my ankle that hurt the most.

"Can you stand?" Mia asked. She helped me to my feet, but putting weight on my ankle was too painful so I immediately sat down again.

"I don't think I can walk," I said.

Panic rose up inside me. This couldn't happen now! What about the farmers' market? What about meeting Mark?

"Where's your phone?" Mia asked. "Let's call the bakery. I don't want to leave you on your own."

I didn't want her to leave me either. I dug out my phone, my hands stinging. Mia took it from me.

"Hi, Paula. It's Mia," she said quickly. "Hannah's hurt – she's fallen over. It's her ankle. We're just up the road but she can't walk. OK, sure. Yeah."

She clicked the phone off. "Paula said to wait here and she'll tell your mum."

"What are we going to do?" I said. I glanced at my watch. It was ten o'clock now. "Mark's waiting for us. I'd better ring him too. Oh, everything's going wrong!" I felt my eyes sting. It wasn't fair. The day was going to be ruined because I hadn't been looking where I was going. Stupid lace. Stupid me. I blinked and tears trickled down my cheeks.

"Don't cry. I can still go!"
Mia said. "As soon as your mum
gets here, I'll go and meet Mark. I can
give out the leaflets and the samples."

"But you said you didn't want to talk to
people," I protested.

"I know." Determination filled Mia's eyes.
"But the bakery needs me to and you need
me to. I'll be fine."

A lady turned into the street and saw me
sitting on the ground. It was Harmony, the
lady who always came into the bakery to talk
about horoscopes with Paula.

"Oh my goodness, Hannah. Are you all
right?" she asked, hurrying over.

I told her I was and that Mum was coming.
Then Neil, the bird-crazy boy, came down
the street and saw me. He came to see if he
could help too.

By the time, Mum ran up the street, we had
three people with us – Harmony, Neil and
another lady on her way to the bakery.

"Hannah, love, what happened?" said
Mum.

I told her about tripping over. She hugged me. "Oh, you poor thing. Come on, let's get you back to the bakery." She thanked everyone.

"I'm going to go to the farmers' market and give out the leaflets," Mia said. She'd texted Mark on my phone to say we'd been a bit delayed. We thought it would be easier for her to explain when she got there.

"OK, thanks." Mum gave her a quick smile.

"I want to go too," I said.

"You can't," said Mum. "You can't walk."

"But . . ."

"No, Hannah." Mum's voice was firm. "You can join Mark and Mia later, if you feel better, but you're coming with me now."

"You can't come to the market like that anyway," said Mia, nodding towards my bleeding palms. "People would run a mile if you tried to give them cake."

I could see she had a point. "Fine," I said. "I'll go back to the bakery and clean up, but then I'm going to the farmers' market."

"We'll see," said Mum.

"Mark and I will be OK," Mia told me. "Don't worry."

She set off at a run, while Mum helped me hobble to the bakery.

Paula was waiting for us at the door. "How are you?" she asked.

"My ankle hurts," I said. I was trying to hold back more tears. I wasn't sure if they were from pain or frustration. I couldn't believe this had happened. I wanted to be at the market. It was amazing of Mia to go without me, it really was, but she was so shy that I wasn't sure she would be much good at convincing people how brilliant the bakery was on her own. And what would happen when Mia saw Misha, Lara and Alice, and realised they were there to help? She'd be so cross with me for not telling her. I gave a strangled sob. It was all such a mess!

Mum took me through to the little staffroom next to the kitchen. She made me lie on the sofa and put my foot up with an ice pack. Then she cleaned my hands and knee and put some antiseptic cream on them.

"Well, I don't think you've broken your ankle," she said, when she found I could wriggle all my toes. "I think it's just twisted. Keep the ice pack on for a bit longer and then I'll strap it up. If it gets any worse, we'll go to the hospital."

"Can I go to the market?" I asked, trying to stand.

"You're not going anywhere right now. Let's see how you're feeling in half an hour. You need to rest. Sit down."

I could tell there was no point arguing. I sat back down heavily. Mum sat beside me and stroked my hair. "It was lucky Mia was with you."

"She was amazing," I agreed, thinking about how calm she'd been. "I thought she'd panic, but she was so brilliant."

"People often surprise us in emergencies," Mum said. She shook her head. "I feel awful. If I'd been organised and got your school uniform like I said, this would never have happened."

"Mum, it's not your fault," I said. I didn't

want her to feel bad. "It could
have happened if I'd been out just
getting some sweets. I should have
done my shoelaces up properly. If it's
anyone's fault, it's mine."

Mum sighed. "No, I shouldn't have let you
go off running around town doing errands.
Particularly when you had such a busy
morning ahead. I could have gone myself
later."

She stroked my hair again. It was lovely,
but I realised that while she was sitting with
me, she wasn't getting any baking done.

"Mum, I'm fine here," I said. "You don't
have to stay. You can get back to baking if
you want."

Mum frowned. "I'm not going to go
and bake while you're sitting here after an
accident. Don't be silly."

"But there's always so much to do."

"You're more important." She took hold of
my hand. "I'm staying right here. There are
plenty of pastries, cakes and muffins in the
counter. It'll be fine."

As I shut my eyes and rested my head against her shoulder, I couldn't stop thinking about the market. Oh please, I thought, I hope it's all OK. Please let me get better so I can find out.

15

In the end, it took a bit longer than half an hour for me to even think about getting up from the sofa. By the time Mum had bandaged my ankle and said she would take me to find Mia and Mark, it was twelve o'clock and Mia and Mark had been there for two hours! I wondered if Alice, Lara and Misha had turned up. And if they had, would Mia still be speaking to me?

The farmers' market was in full swing when we arrived. Colourful stalls with brightly striped awnings filled the square. There were people selling meats, chutneys, pies, wine, cheeses, herbs and vegetables, as customers enjoyed the sights, sounds and tastes of the market.

I scanned the stalls. Where were Mark and Mia?

"There they are!" Mum said.

I followed her gaze and spotted Mark handing out leaflets and Mia passing around a plate filled with samples of cake. She was chatting to people and smiling. And there were Alice, Misha and Lara too! They also had leaflets and plates in their hands.

I limped over, waving.

"Hannah!" cried Alice.

"Would you like to try some of the Sugar and Spice Bakery's delicious lemon cake, madam?" Misha said, shoving a plate of samples under my nose.

"Or chocolate cake," said Lara, joining her.

I looked across at Mia who was talking to a customer near the stall. She flashed a grin in my direction and a surreptitious thumbs-up. She didn't look cross at all, just happy.

"Mia told us what had happened," said Alice, as Mum went to see Mark. "Is your ankle OK?"

"Just twisted," I said. "But it was so painful. I haven't been able to move until just now. I'm really sorry I left you all to it."

"Luckily for you, the Dream Team have been here to save the day!" said Misha. "I think everyone in the market knows about the Sugar and Spice Bakery now!"

"These cakes are really delicious," said Lara.

"You're not supposed to eat them yourself, greedy guts," said Misha, nudging her.

"Everyone has one piece and then comes back for more," said Alice.

I looked around at them. "Thanks so much for helping," I said. "I was really worried. Mia doesn't like talking to strangers."

"She seems to be doing all right now," said Alice, nodding to where Mia was chatting to another person and giving them a leaflet.

Misha grinned at me. "You were right – she *is* different when you get to know her."

"She seemed a bit surprised to see us when we got here," said Lara. "But I think she was just glad of the help. She told us what to do and gave us the samples to hand out and we've been busy ever since."

"It's been loads of fun," said Misha. "In fact, I think I've got a natural talent for it!" She ran after a man passing by. "Sir, I'm sure you'd like to try a piece of lemon cake, wouldn't you?" she said. "It's absolutely delicious and completely free! It's from the Sugar and Spice Bakery."

"A brand new bakery that's just opened in town on Parson's Lane," Alice added. "It's a family-owned business and the cakes are the best in the world!"

The man smiled. "Well, I'd better try a piece and see if I agree."

He took a piece of cake and nodded appreciatively.

"Have a leaflet," said Lara. "There's a voucher for a free cup of coffee when you come in."

"Thank you," he said. "I'll certainly stop by. This is delicious cake."

He walked off. Misha, Lara and Alice high-fived.

I turned around to see Mia talking to a family and handing them a leaflet.

My new friends, I thought, looking around at the four of them. Maybe living in Ashingham was going to be OK after all.

The next few hours flew by. Once she saw I was all right, Mum went back to the bakery, making Mark promise to ring her if I started to look tired. She was delighted to see so many people enthusing over her cakes.

"We might even be busy this afternoon," she said, her eyes dancing with hope.

By two o'clock, we'd run out of cake *and* leaflets, so we packed up. Mark offered to drop Alice, Misha and Lara home, but they said they would walk.

"See you at school on Monday," Misha said.

"Yeah." I smiled. Suddenly the thought of school didn't knot up my stomach and make me feel sick. I realised I was actually looking forward to it.

"Should I call for you and we can walk in together on Monday morning?" said Alice.

I glanced at Mia. "I was going to walk in with Mia."

Alice smiled. "So, let's all go together. If you want to, Mia?"

Mia's eyes lit up. "Yes – great."

"See you both on Monday, then!" Alice said, waving.

As soon as they were out of earshot I turned to Mia.

"So?" I said teasingly. "Do you still not want to be friends with them?"

She grinned. "Maybe I've changed my mind."

"What happened?" I asked.

"They just turned up," Mia said. She glanced at me and a slightly accusing tone crept into her voice. "They said you'd asked them to help."

I blushed. "I'm sorry," I told her. "I should have said. I—"

"It's OK," said Mia. "I get why you didn't tell me and I don't mind. Really I don't. It's funny – it was so hectic I didn't have time to feel shy. I just told them what to do. And then once we started giving out the samples, I realised you were right. They're nice."

I beamed. "Told you!" I said.

163

Mark dropped Mia home and then insisted I lie on the sofa to rest my ankle before the cake sale the next day. I snuggled under a blanket with some magazines, thinking about everything that had happened. At around five o'clock, I heard Mum come in.

"How are you feeling, sweetie?" she asked, popping her head around the door.

"Fine," I said. "Actually, better than fine." I'd been enjoying lying on the sofa, reading. Life had been so busy recently, it had been ages since I'd just lazed around.

"Good." Mum paused. "Well . . . aren't you going to ask me how the bakery was this afternoon?"

"How was it?" I asked in surprise.

"Busy!" Mum heaved a huge, happy sigh. "We had loads of people come in with those free coffee vouchers and they all bought something to eat too. It was such a good idea, Hannah. We sold out – we didn't have a cake or muffin left!"

"Oh, Mum, that's brilliant!" I said.

She hugged me. "To celebrate I'm going to

go and make a chicken pie for us all."

"Yum!" Mum's chicken pie is my all-time favourite meal.

Mum shook her head. "It's strange. I never thought I'd do LESS baking at home now I have the bakery, but then quite a lot of things are different from how I'd imagined."

"You are glad you opened it, aren't you?" I asked.

"Of course," she said. "I knew it would be hard work but I hadn't realised quite how much there would be to do. Or how tired I'd be. There's so much to think about all the time – it's not just the baking." She glanced at me. "I'm sorry."

I frowned. "What for?"

"For not being around for you more." She sat next to me and put her arm around my shoulders. "For relying on you to cope. For forgetting you're only ten and for being so caught up in the bakery." She shook her head and spoke half to herself. "Things are going to have to change. We can't go on like this."

"What do you mean?" I said.

Mum kissed me and stood up. "I'll tell you about my ideas later. I need to have a chat with Mark first and see what he thinks, but today has made me think the bakery really might be a success. I think we're going to be OK."

"I bet we'll have loads more customers," I said. "Everyone from today will tell their friends and families, and we'll have more and more regulars."

Mum's eyes glowed. "That would be wonderful!"

I leaned back against the sofa. I loved the bakery, the food Mum made, the people I'd met – Paula, Mia, Alice, Mrs Rees and the customers I was getting to know. The bakery was more than just a business. It was a place I loved going to and I wanted it to be a huge success.

Mum smiled happily. "It's onwards and upwards from here on. I'm sure of it. Now, you get some rest. I'll call you when supper's ready."

I lay on the sofa, wondering what Mum had meant about things changing. After a while I heard Mark go out to fetch the twins from their gran's. When they got back, I could tell he'd told them about my accident because, as soon as they had taken their shoes and coats off, they came charging into the lounge.

"What happened?" said Molly.

"Can I see your bandage?" said Ella.

"I just fell over and hurt my ankle. Look."

"If I had a bandage I'd want it to be pink," said Molly, inspecting it. "White's boring."

"Poor Hannah," said Ella. She whispered something to Molly and they both ran away. Five minutes later they were back, dragging Little Mermaid suitcases packed with a *Scooby Doo* annual, colouring pens, a Disney princess colouring book, a pink tiara and several cuddly toys.

"These are for you," said Ella. "From us."

I looked at their little faces and felt a warm glow. OK, they could be a pain, but I was suddenly really glad that Mum had married

Mark and Molly and Ella had come to live with us.

I read them stories until Mum called us for dinner. We sat in the dining room for the first time since we'd moved here. There were pots filled with steaming vegetables – bright orange carrots, sweet green peas and creamy mashed potatoes. In the middle of the table was a big chicken pie with a golden crust and a jug full of gravy beside it.

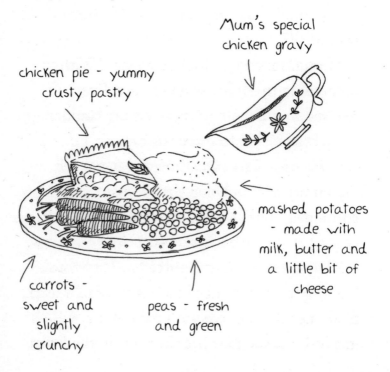

Mum's special chicken gravy

chicken pie - yummy crusty pastry

mashed potatoes - made with milk, butter and a little bit of cheese

carrots - sweet and slightly crunchy

peas - fresh and green

As Mum cut into the pie, deliciously scented steam rushed out, and she divided it between our plates.

"Dig in!" she said.

Soon we were all passing the vegetables and pouring drinks. It felt great to be together after such an incredible, but tiring, day.

At last I couldn't eat another mouthful. "I'm stuffed!" I said.

"So," Mark looked at Mum. "Are you going to tell Hannah what you've been thinking?"

Mum nodded and looked at me. "With everything that's happened today, I've realised that I can't go on like this, Hannah. I need to be able to leave the bakery. I don't want to be tired all the time and never see my family. I've decided that if business continues to be as good as it was today, I'm going to take on an apprentice. As you know, Paula knows an eighteen-year-old lad who's looking for experience in a bakery. He'll learn from me and help me with the baking, which means I can spend more time out in the front of the shop, and hopefully I'll be able to take half-days sometimes so I can be here when you get home from school."

"That's brilliant!" I said.

"There needs to be more of a balance in my life," said Mum.

I grinned. "Like in a cake."

"Exactly," she said. "It's like a carrot cake. It needs a whole mixture of things to make it perfect – sugar, carrots, a pinch of nutmeg and cinnamon. It needs both sugar and spice." Our eyes met and we smiled. "Of course, we'll have to keep up the advertising to make sure we get customers in," she continued. "But I hope you can help me with that. You've got a knack for it. The farmers' market was a really great idea."

"And the leaflets," added Mark.

"Having an apprentice will mean I'm able to spend more time with you, baking and, of course, designing cakes," Mum said. "What do you think?"

I looked at my bandaged foot. "I think I'm very glad I fell over today!" I said. The day might have started disastrously but it had turned out better than I could have ever hoped. Now we just had to make a success of the cake stall tomorrow. Oh, I hoped we would. It would be . . . well, the icing on the cake!

16

Well, what can I say about the cake sale apart
from that it was A-MA-ZING! There were
lots of people to cheer the belly dancers on as
they danced hour after hour. And everyone
LOVED our cakes and biscuits. Mrs Rees
arrived with a few of her dog-walking
friends, and Paula made sure that everyone
she knew (which was basically the whole
of Ashingham) had heard about the event.
Alice, Lara and Misha couldn't be there
because they had to go to something called a
gymkhana at their riding stables, but they all
texted to wish me and Mia luck.

Mia came round to my house early so we
could ice the cakes and biscuits together, and

Mum showed us how to make little flowers to decorate them. The cakes looked brilliant – some with swirly piped rich buttercream icing and others with royal icing in pale shades of pink and green.

It was the best afternoon I'd had since moving. It was lovely to spend time with Mum, doing things like this. I realised how much I'd missed it. And having Mia there was great because she loved it as much as I did.

When we finally went to the hall and opened our stall, the money poured in. Everyone knew we were selling the cakes to raise money for Tom, so lots of people told us to keep the change or paid us more than the price tags. A TV crew from the local news even arrived and took some film of the dancers and interviewed Paula while she danced.

1. Have lots of money to use as change.
2. Label all the things you're selling and put prices on.
3. Have paper bags or plates and cling film in case people want to take cakes home.
4. Have a list of ingredients used in all the different cakes – some people with food allergies might want to know what is in them.

By the time the belly dancing ended, we had sold out of everything. There was a huge cheer as the belly dance finished and then Paula came over to us. She was bright red and her short dark hair was sticking up even more than normal.

"We did it!" she said, sinking on to a chair. "We survived and we've raised loads of money."

"And the girls have raised plenty too," said Mum, holding up the plastic tub where we'd been keeping the money. "There's over three hundred pounds in here."

Paula gasped. "That's wonderful!"

"And, hopefully, if people see the news on TV tonight it will raise awareness too. We'll put a donations box in the bakery," said Mum.

Paula smiled at us. "Thank you so much, girls."

"It was fun," said Mia.

Paula heaved herself up from the chair. "I'm going to be stiff as a board tomorrow!" She spotted someone across the room and waved. "There's my sister – Tom's mum! And my niece! Wait till I tell them how much you raised. They'll be so grateful. Yoo-hoo!" she shouted. "Lisa! Tegan!"

TEGAN?

Mia and I swung around. Tegan was coming towards us. She was wearing black jeans and biker boots, and she was chewing gum. She didn't look happy to be there. With her was a lady who looked like a younger version of Paula. *Tegan* was Paula's niece!

Suddenly I could see the family resemblance, but Tegan – horrible Tegan – being lovely Paula's niece just didn't seem right. I looked at Mia. All the happy glow had drained from her face. I stepped in front of her protectively.

"Tegan's really struggling with Tom's illness," I heard Paula murmur to Mum. "She used to be such a sweet girl, but she keeps getting into trouble at the moment. I think it's a mixture of attention seeking and just feeling desperate that she can't do anything to help Tom. They've always been close."

"It must be tough for her," Mum said sympathetically.

I glanced at Mia again. She was gazing at Tegan like a frightened rabbit.

"Lisa. This is Rose, who owns the bakery," said Paula, when Tegan and her mum arrived at the stall. "And this is her daughter, Hannah, and Hannah's friend, Mia." I saw Tegan's look of surprise. "Hannah and Mia had the idea of running the cake stall," Paula went on. "They've raised over three hundred pounds."

Lisa beamed. "Oh, that's wonderful. I can't tell you how grateful we are, girls."

"You're welcome." I smiled but I was watching Tegan. There was a strange expression on her face, as if she couldn't work out what to say. Lisa and Paula chatted to Mum about the bakery, leaving Tegan standing awkwardly with us.

"You raised all that money for my brother?" she said eventually.

I nodded. "Yeah."

Tegan's frown deepened. "Why?"

"Because we wanted to help," I said. I took a breath and met her gaze. "Mia's been brilliant. It was all her idea."

Mia was staring at the ground.

"*Your* idea?" Tegan looked at Mia, as if seeing her for the first time.

I stared from one to the other. I hated the way Tegan had been treating Mia but she looked so sad that I suddenly felt really sorry for her.

"It must be tough having a brother who's so ill," I said.

Tegan didn't reply. I saw a muscle clench in her jaw.

"We're glad we could help a bit," I said. "Aren't we, Mia?"

"Yep!" Mia's voice was high. "We really are."

"Come on, T," Lisa called. "We should get home and see how Tom is. He wanted to come today, but he wasn't feeling too good," she told my mum.

"I hope you've raised enough money," Mum said. "Let us know if there's anything else we can do to help."

"Thanks," said Lisa. They smiled at each other, and then Lisa and Tegan started to walk away with Paula.

Mia was very quiet as she and I started to clear up. We were just packing up the last few bits from the stall when Tegan came striding towards us. She reached into the pocket of her jeans. "Look . . . thanks," she said brusquely, shoving something into Mia's hand.

Mia gaped at her in surprise before Tegan marched away. She looked at me and held out her hand. In it was exactly £1.20.

"Did that just happen?" Mia whispered to me. "Did Tegan McGarrity just say thank you and give me my money back?"

"I think she did," I said.

"What does it mean?" Mia said.

I shrugged.

"Who knows?" I looked in Tegan's direction. She turned and gave us a brief smile. "But I think it might be good."

The hall was emptying. We finished packing away and helped Mum load up the car.

"Hop in," Mark said, opening the door for us.

I got in the back beside Mia and grinned at her.

"What?" she said, grinning back.

"Nothing. Just that I'm glad you came into the bakery and I met you."

She smiled back. "Me too."

As Mark drove us home I looked out of the window and thought about the new friends I had made in the last week. I thought about how often we judge people by looking at the surface, even though that's not fair. There are people like Alice who seem lovely at first sight and who *are* lovely – they're

the human versions of
cupcakes with sugar
flowers on top. Then there
are other people, who are
more like pancake batter
or sourdough starter.
Perhaps they don't appear
to be anything special at first
sight, you might

not even be sure you'll like them, but they
can surprise you. Sometimes REALLY
surprise you – like Mia. She'd been amazing
the last few days – coming up with the idea
for the cake stall, staying so calm when I
fell over, handing out the leaflets and samples
at the farmers' market with Alice, Lara and
Misha, even though she'd been really worried
about it. I suddenly realised that, if I had
to pick something from the bakery to
compare her to, it would be Mum's incredible
sourdough. Nothing flashy, easily overlooked
in a way, but totally, deep down awesome!

Maybe thinking of everyone I meet as some
sort of bakery product makes me sound a

bit weird. But as we pass the bakery, with the last rays of the sun lighting up the shop window and I think how many friends I've met through the bakery and how many more people I might meet there, you know what? I'm very glad to be me!

the orion star

★ ★ ★